He knew he shouldn't be kissing her.

And yet he needed this. At this moment he felt like he couldn't do without it.

She was something, this woman. Strong and determined, yet with a tender heart. What he wouldn't give to stay in her arms, to make her his. To wake every day to a woman like this. To let her be his reason for living.

But he was a sheik from a foreign land and she was a Wyoming cowgirl. It was an impossible dream.

Efraim ended the kiss and looked down. He knew he should feel ashamed, that he should regret it. But he'd never regret kissing Callie.

No matter what happened.

D0836429

ANN VOSS PETERSON

SEIZED BY THE SHEIK

TORONTO NEW YORK LONDON
AMSTERDAM PARIS SYDNEY HAMBURG
STOCKHOLM ATHENS TOKYO MILAN MADRID
PRAGUE WARSAW BUDAPEST AUCKLAND

To everyone who chooses tolerance and love over hate and fear.

Special thanks and acknowledgment to Ann Voss Peterson for her
contribution to the Cowboys Royale series.

Recycling programs
for this product may
not exist in your area.

ISBN-13: 978-0-373-69524-9

SEIZED BY THE SHEIK

www.eHarlequin.com

Printed in U.S.A.

ABOUT THE AUTHOR

Ever since she was a little girl making her own books out of construction paper, Ann Voss Peterson wanted to write. So when it came time to choose a major at the University of Wisconsin, creative writing was her only choice. Of course, writing wasn't a *practical* choice—one needs to earn a living. So Ann found jobs, including proofreading legal transcripts, working with quarter horses and washing windows. But no matter how she earned her paycheck, she continued to write the type of stories that captured her heart and imagination— romantic suspense. Ann lives near Madison, Wisconsin, with her husband, her two young sons, her border collie and her quarter horse mare. Ann loves to hear from readers. Email her at ann@annvosspeterson.com or visit her website at www.annvosspeterson.com.

Books by Ann Voss Peterson

HARLEQUIN INTRIGUE
745—BOYS IN BLUE
    "LIAM"
780—LEGALLY BINDING
838—DESERT SONS
    "TOM"
878—MARITAL PRIVILEGE
925—SERIAL BRIDE*
931—EVIDENCE OF MARRIAGE*
937—VOW TO PROTECT*
952—CRITICAL EXPOSURE
981—SPECIAL ASSIGNMENT
1049—WYOMING MANHUNT
1095—CHRISTMAS AWAKENING
1133—PRICELESS NEWBORN PRINCE
1160—COVERT COOTCHIE-COOTCHIE-COO
1202—ROCKY MOUNTAIN FUGITIVE
1220—A RANCHER'S BRAND OF JUSTICE
1238—A COP IN HER STOCKING
1257—SEIZED BY THE SHEIK

*Wedding Mission

CAST OF CHARACTERS

Efraim Aziz—A sheik from the small island nation of Nadar, Efraim doesn't trust the United States or anyone in it. That is, until he meets Callie McGuire.

Callie McGuire—An assistant to the U.S. Secretary of Foreign Affairs, Callie dreams of finding a man who accepts both sides of her—the world-traveling diplomat and the all-American girl who grew up on a Wyoming ranch.

Fahad Bahir—The man would go to great lengths to protect his cousin, Sheik Efraim, and the interests of his beloved country of Nadar.

Clay McGuire—Callie's father wants her to settle down, but a sheik isn't the man he would choose for his only daughter. How far will he go to prevent the match?

Brent McGuire—Callie's older brother is a hothead with anger issues. How far would he go to protect his sister from the man he sees as a threat?

Russ McGuire—Little brother Russ likes to follow Brent's lead in all things except women. There he is in a league of his own. But this time, has a woman led him astray?

Timmy McGuire—The youngest McGuire sibling is only in high school, and when he's attacked, the whole family rushes to his aid.

Kateb Bahir—Kateb competes with his older brother in all things. Did sibling rivalry finally turn to violence?

Tanya Driscoll—Does the party girl simply want a good time? Or is she after something more serious...and deadly?

Chapter One

The place felt like death.

Efraim Aziz lowered his rein hand and let his horse pick his own path through the acres-wide gash of eroded red-and-beige rock. Wind whistled through the formations and battered his face, incessant and strong. A few sticks of sagebrush twisted through kinks in the rock to stretch their silver-green leaves to the sky, the only living thing for what looked like miles. These badlands, the high plains, the mountain ranges to the west and north—it was a harsh landscape populated by hard, arrogant people. And somewhere in this hell Amir Khalid was struggling, dying...if he wasn't already dead.

Efraim had to find his friend.

"Sheik Efraim! Wait!"

He recognized the voice immediately, its sound shivering over his skin like the warm breath of a lover. He knew someone would come looking for him, but he'd never guessed it would be her.

He glanced over his shoulder.

She rode toward him through the badlands astride a palomino quarter horse. Her long blond hair glimmered in the Wyoming sun like the golden beaches of his island nation of Nadar.

Efraim tried his best to ignore the spike in his blood pressure, the acceleration of his pulse.

He didn't even know her, this Callie McGuire. They'd engaged in a few polite discussions when he'd arrived in America, and only glances in the stressful days since. But whenever she was near, he had a hard time keeping his eyes off her. It was as if she was the only person in the room. Magnetic. And as hot as the sun itself.

Whoever sent *her* to collect him was shrewd, indeed.

"Sheik Efraim. Please."

He scooped in a deep breath of hot horse and leather and braced himself before turning his mount back to face her.

She'd come to talk him into going back, holing up like a coward. And even though he didn't intend to follow her advice, he knew he would listen to her every word with the attentiveness of a teenage boy enslaved to his hormones. Embarrassing for the leader of a country. Shameful.

She came to a halt in front of him, but her eyes darted around, taking in the sagebrush, the crumbled rock outcroppings, the mountains on the horizon. "Where's your security?"

He thought of his cousin Fahad and the men who worked under him. "At the Wind River Ranch."

"You're out here without protection?"

"Who sent you after me? Fahad?"

"I like to ride, clear my head." She gave him a doe-eyed look, all innocence.

A sure sign he was being handled.

He raised a brow. "So is this the job you expected when you chose to work for your country's Office of Foreign Affairs? Babysitter?"

She rested her rein hand on the saddle horn, her blue eyes squinted against the glare. "You shouldn't be out here, sir. It's too dangerous. Whoever planted that car bomb to kill Sheik Amir will be trying to kill you, too."

"So Fahad did send you. My head of security?" Efraim knew it. Kateb must have run to his brother this morning as soon as he'd trailered Efraim and one of the Wind River Ranch's horses to the rural road where the explosion had occurred.

"I haven't heard from Mr. Bahir." She let out a breath, as if giving up. "Actually I was hoping he was out here keeping an eye on you."

"Yes, I wouldn't be surprised if he is." Efraim took his own glance around the landscape but saw no sign of his cousin. "So if it wasn't Fahad, who sent you?"

"That's not important."

"It is to me." He wasn't sure if he was more disturbed by the thought that someone believed Callie McGuire could protect him better than he could protect himself, or by the indication that whoever had sent her knew of his powerful attraction for the fresh-faced blonde.

If it was one of his men, he'd be on the next plane back to Nadar.

"You need to head back to the resort. Sunset comes early in these parts because of the mountains." She stared him down, her jaw as set and determined as it had been yesterday.

That was it. Her jaw. The flash in her eyes. That was what drew him. He was a sucker for strong women. Being from a country where women weren't allowed to be strong around men, this feistiness was novel and obviously the source of his fascination with Callie McGuire. "You're worried about me?" he said in a dry tone, but he couldn't pretend there wasn't a note of teasing interest under his words.

"You're very important to the coalition."

In the past few weeks, he'd heard enough about the Coalition of Island Nations, or COIN, to last him a lifetime. He wasn't even sure it was in Nadar's best interest to be part of it. With each day that had passed since the explosion, his doubts had grown. "Nadar's offshore oil fields are important to the coalition. The shipping lanes are important to the coalition. Not me."

"Then why did Prince Stefan call me?"

So it had been Stefan Lutece who'd thought he needed a babysitter and had chosen Callie McGuire for the job. Humiliating that the Prince of Kyros could see his interest so clearly, but at least he wasn't a subordinate. "He shouldn't have bothered you."

"If anyone knows about the dangers all the members of the coalition face, it's Prince Stefan."

"Or Amir. And finding him is why I'm here."

"You think you're going to find some sign of him out here on the BLM?" She gestured to the surroundings with her free hand.

As Efraim understood it, the barren canyonlike area he was now searching in was called Rattlesnake Badlands, a part of public land controlled by the Bureau of

Land Management. The locals just referred to all of it as the BLM.

"I'm not going to cower at some luxury resort ranch while Amir might be out here dying."

"There are people searching."

"Who? The police? Some honest ones, or just the ones taking money from organized crime?"

She scrunched up her nose, and he noticed for the first time that she had a sprinkle of freckles across the top of her cheekbones. Fascinating.

He concentrated on a large clump of sage just past her right ear. "Amir didn't disappear. He has to be somewhere."

"So don't rely on the authorities. Let your own people do the job. You don't have to do this personally."

But he did. It was that or go crazy. The Wind River Ranch and Resort was a luxurious place, that was for certain, but he couldn't enjoy it knowing Amir was out there, maybe dying, maybe dead. "There's no argument you can make that Fahad has not already made."

The hard line of her lips softened. "I know the two of you are close. I know you're worried about him."

Whereas her passion had been arousing, the softness and empathy in her eyes mesmerized him and for a moment, he found himself physically leaning toward her in his saddle.

He caught himself before he swooned like a lovesick teen. "When Amir is found, I will stop searching." He laid a spur to his horse's side, and the animal broke into a jog. He wasn't wild about much of what America had to offer, but he might make an exception for its quarter horses and its women.

At least *this* woman.

"Then I'll help—"

A gunshot cracked through the air, cutting her sentence short.

Efraim grabbed for his pistol and tried to gauge where the shot came from. The report bounced off rock and mixed with the whistle of the wind.

So much for finding Amir. Hemmed in by canyon walls, he and Callie would be lucky if they got out of the Rattlesnake Badlands alive.

Chapter Two

Pulse pounding so hard that her hands shook, Callie pulled her prize rifle from the scabbard on her saddle. Her throat felt as dry as the dust under their horses' hooves. What was she thinking, rushing out here without bringing the sheik's security detail with her? How did she think she and a rifle were going to stack up against the forces out there who would do anything to stop the COIN summit from taking place? When she'd gotten the call from Prince Stefan, she'd been confident she could talk Efraim into returning to the ranch. She hadn't given an extra thought to what she would do if they suddenly found themselves in a war zone. "We need to get out of here."

"We need to make ourselves smaller targets." Sheik Efraim threw a leg back over the saddle and slid to the ground. "The echoes. Can you tell where the shot came from?"

Her boots hit the ground. The crazy way the sound bounced off the canyon walls made finding the source nearly impossible. She pointed in the direction she thought she'd first heard the sound. "There. Can't tell for sure."

He gestured to a formation, and they slipped behind it. Walls of red-and-tan rock rose around them. A miniature version of a box canyon. Safe, but only until the shooter decided to block off the only escape route.

"We can't stay here," Callie whispered. "They had to have seen where we went. We'll be trapped."

"I'm not planning to stay." He squinted into the sun. Lines fanned out from the corners of his eyes. He looked concerned, yet calm. A man used to being in tight places. "Do you have a phone?"

"No reception out here."

"What's closest? Town?"

She shook her head. Dumont was a good distance by foot or by horse. Even the ranch owned by family friend Helen Jefferies would take an awfully long time to reach through this canyon. Faster to get out of Rattlesnake Badlands as quickly as possible and head in the other direction. "My family's ranch is closest. If we exit the canyon to the south, we can probably make it by nightfall."

The sheik arched his black brows. "Your family?"

"I grew up here." For some reason, she'd assumed he knew that. Strange. But every time he looked at her, it felt like his dark eyes saw everything. Her innermost thoughts and feelings. Even her past.

"Then you know the land."

"Yes. Any ideas who is shooting at us?" She'd like to think it was a local out shooting targets on the BLM, something she and her brothers did more times than she could count. But she knew that was unlikely at best.

"Russian mob? That might give us some room to work."

"Room to work?" That was her worst fear. A sniper like the one who had tried to kill Prince Stefan. A man whose aim was to kill, ruthlessly, and who had the skill to pull it off.

"He probably doesn't know the area. Not like you do."

A silver lining, if only a shred of one. "You're right. So we have an advantage there."

"We sure don't have one in firepower." He held up his pistol. A nice weapon, but not much use at a distance. "Are you a good shot?"

"Won some shooting contests when I was in high school." She held up her rifle, showing him the brass plaque on the stock proclaiming her Wind River County Champion Marksman, Junior Women's Division. The whole idea of shooting competitions seemed ridiculous and trivial in light of the situation they were in. Fun and games in the face of life and death.

He nodded, as if it was exactly what he was hoping for. "Okay. Then you can cover me." He handed her his horse's reins.

His words jolted her like a slap. "Cover you? Where are you going?"

"That first shot, it wasn't meant for us."

"Who was it meant for?"

"Whoever is up on that ridge." He pointed across a rough area of the canyon floor to a ridge of rock. "See him?"

She shielded her eyes with her hand.

"To the right. You can see something white, a sleeve." Lightly touching her cheek, he tilted her face in the correct direction.

She tried not to think about the feel of his touch and focus on spotting what he was trying to show her. Sure enough, some sort of white cloth was flapping in the wind. "I see it. You think it's a person?"

"I think it's a body."

"You saw him get shot?"

"Not exactly. I didn't realize he was there. Not until after the shot was fired and he suddenly wasn't."

"And you plan to climb up there?"

"We can't leave him."

"Do you know who it is?"

He shook his head. "Let's hope not." Holding his weapon at the ready, he stepped forward.

"Wait." She grabbed his shoulder. "If this is a sniper…"

He looked back. His eyes fixed on hers. "That's why I'm relying on you. Can you cover me?"

Her insides shook so badly that she didn't even know if she could manage to get her finger to the trigger. The dossier she'd studied on his background had mentioned military service, as with the other COIN leaders. But even though she'd grown up around guns and knew the terrain, she was no soldier. At the sound of that first gunshot, adrenaline had hollowed out her stomach and turned the rest of her into a quivering mess.

He leaned toward her, closer than a man had been in a long while, and tapped on the award plaque on her rifle stock. "You'll be fine."

She nodded, even though she wasn't so sure. She squinted up at the ridge and the wisp of white fabric flapping in the wind like a flag of surrender.

"Wait." She stepped to her mare's side and rummaged

through the saddlebags with her free hand. Her fingers touched the pair of binoculars she had used to find the sheik. She pulled them out and handed them to him. "You should be able to see the area better from up there, maybe spot our shooter."

"Good thinking."

She shouldn't feel so warm at his praise, but she couldn't deny the flicker in her chest. A flicker that for a moment eclipsed the shaking. She stood up a little straighter. "Please be careful, Sheik Efraim."

"Just Efraim. Please."

"Efraim. Be careful."

He nodded. Pistol in front of him, he started climbing up through the eroded and crumbling rock.

She shouldered the rifle and scanned the area through the scope. She'd ridden out here to bring him back to the Wind River Ranch, and that's what she'd do. If there was one thing her daddy taught her, it was to do what needed to be done.

A lesson that had served her well so far.

The crunch and scrape of his footsteps faded into the wind. She forced herself to breathe, stay steady and alert. Next to her, Efraim's horse tossed his head. Her mare, Sasha, pawed the ground.

"Callie," Efraim called, his voice rasping, as if his throat was filled with sand.

She lowered the rifle slightly and glanced up.

His dark head peeked over the edge of the cliff, bent over the body they'd seen from below. "I need your help."

"I'll be right there."

"Can you find a way to get the horses up here?"

She tried to picture the canyon in her mind's eye. If she wound south, the slope was more gentle. The horses should be able to handle it. "I think so."

"I'll cover you as best I can. Hurry."

Tucking her rifle back in its scabbard, she grasped the reins and started trudging in a wide arc that sloped up to the canyon's edge. Whoever Efraim found up on that cliff must be hurt, not dead. And knowing that gave her a little more hope that all this would turn out okay.

The trek seemed to take forever. But except for a few slips and scrambles of steel shoes on hard rock, the horses plugged along. She turned the last corner, the point that should bring her to the level where Efraim crouched by the body. A rock face loomed in front of her.

She let out a heavy breath.

It wasn't high, only about ten feet of jumbled rock rising to a wider cap formation on top called a hoodoo. But small or not, the barrier was squarely between her and Efraim.

She could climb the side and skirt around the saddle-horn-shaped hoodoo with a little effort, but the horses couldn't.

She glanced around, her gaze landing on a scraggle of half-dead sagebrush. Sasha was trained to ground tie with the best of them. She wasn't so confident about the horse from the Wind River Ranch. Without a sturdy halter and lead, she couldn't tie the animal very securely, but maybe it would be enough.

She looped the horse's reins around the woody base of the sage. She dropped Sasha's reins free next to it. "Whoa." As long as something didn't happen, they should be fine.

Turning back to the rocky face, she spied Efraim staring down at her. He cupped his hand around his mouth. "Do you have something plastic? A bag? Something like that?"

Her mind raced, trying to decipher the reason behind the request. She turned back to her horse. She kept a number of things with her when riding out on the ranch or the BLM, but plastic bags weren't among them. She returned to Sasha and grabbed the saddlebags from the saddle. Pausing, she grabbed the rain slicker she'd tied on the saddle's skirt and carried all back to the swell of rock and started climbing.

Loose sand and stones skittered under her feet. She slipped twice, trying to catch herself with hands weighed down with saddlebags and slicker. A rock face about three feet high formed the final hurdle. But from here she could clearly see Efraim and the white fabric they'd spotted from the canyon floor.

It wasn't a shirt, as she'd previously thought, but a traditional head cloth designed to protect the wearer from the harsh sun.

The kind of sun that beat down on the island of Nadar.

A chill fanned over Callie's skin despite the June heat. She focused on Efraim. "One of your people?"

Efraim looked up, dark eyes glistening. Rusty red smeared his cheekbone where he'd swiped at his eyes with a bloody hand. "It's Fahad."

NUMBNESS PENETRATED bone deep. When Efraim first realized the body lying on the canyon's edge was Fahad, he'd almost staggered under the blow. Then training had kicked in. Cold, methodical. His cousin was badly injured, but alive. Callie and he were in danger. It was up to him to get them all to safety before it was too late.

Fahad stared at him with dark eyes and open mouth, struggling for oxygen. With each breath, a sucking sound emanated from his chest wound. Efraim pressed his wadded-up shirt against the wound. Within seconds it was soaked with blood, warm and sticky on his hands. The sound continued.

He looked up at Callie, climbing the last few feet of rock-strewn slope. "Plastic?"

"I have a slicker and some first-aid supplies." She held up a bundle cradled in her arms.

He needed those supplies. And she couldn't climb the last rock wall while carrying them. He rose to his feet to take them from her.

A second shot split the air. Rock exploded next to his face.

Efraim hit the deck. His foot hit Fahad's rifle, sending it careening into the canyon. Still climbing the rocky slope, Callie flattened. Beyond her, a horse whinnied. Steel shoes clattered on stone.

The horses. They were running away.

Keeping low to the ground this time, Efraim crawled to the slope. His thoughts raced. The shot had hit the stone near him, Callie had to be merely taking cover. She had to be okay.

Reaching the edge, he peered over.

She looked up at him, her freckles streaked by dust, her blue eyes wide. "Here." She pushed the bundle toward him.

He took the saddle bags and slicker. "Stay low."

"I'll climb up. I can help."

"No." The last thing he wanted was for Callie to attempt to climb the ridge and get shot for her efforts. "I'll tend to Fahad, then you can help me move him."

He moved back to Fahad's side. His cousin was still conscious, still fighting. He moved his lips, but no sound came, just the sucking noise mixed with each gasp for breath.

"Hold on. I have supplies. It will be all right."

His cousin gave a light bob of the head.

Efraim folded the slicker and pulled an elastic bandage from the saddlebags. He wasn't sure this was going to work, but he did know that if he did nothing, Fahad would die.

He had ripped Fahad's shirt open as soon as he'd found him. Now he pushed the tattered and bloody fabric aside and pressed the slick side of the raincoat against the wound. Grasping the bandage roll in sticky hands, he strapped it across Fahad's chest, fitting the slicker tight against his skin. It was far from sterile, far from ideal, but it was the best he could do. He just prayed it would work.

Something scraped rock and Callie slipped to her knees by his side.

"I told you to stay—"

"It will go faster with both of us."

He shook his head and peered down at the badlands below. "You have to go back down the slope."

"I know you're trying to protect me. But faster is better. For Fahad and for both of us." She set her chin and gripped Fahad's shoulders. "Now, are you going to help me sit him up or not?"

He helped her tilt Fahad toward him. Callie wrapped the rest of the slicker around his side and over the exit wound in his back. They wrapped the bandage around his chest, securing the slicker as tightly as possible to the wound.

Fahad gasped again and again, but this time he seemed to be getting air. Tears leaked from the corners of his eyes and trickled down the side of his face and into his beard. Beads of sweat bloomed on his forehead.

"Fahad, who did this?" Efraim asked.

"Followed you."

"Who?"

He shook his head, the movement barely perceptible. "Don't know."

Efraim's pulse beat in his ears, loud as gunfire. Any second another shot could crack through the canyon, a bullet could plow into one of them and end it all.

"Have you spotted the shooter?" Callie asked.

He took a quick glance around the canyon formations. Between the hoodoos, crumbled cliffs and pocks of vegetation, he couldn't pick out the form of a man. All he had to go on was the trajectory of the shot that had missed his head. "I think he's to the north. And I think he's somewhat below us because he didn't see me until I stood."

"Your horse. The gunshot spooked him."

He glanced up. He'd assumed both horses had run. "Just mine?"

She nodded. "I've competed in shooting competitions on horseback, too. Sasha's used to it. She's waiting at the bottom of the slope."

He let out a breath. At least one thing had gone

right in all this. They'd need a horse if they hoped to get Fahad out of here and to someone who could help him.

"The horse will probably head for one of the ranches around here. My dad's. Helen's. He'll be all right."

Efraim hadn't been thinking of the horse. He'd been more concerned about their being all right. But he gave her a nod all the same.

Callie grabbed another bandage from the saddlebags, this one a self-adhesive horse wrap. They wrapped until they'd covered Fahad's back and shoulder.

Now came the tricky part. "We need to move him, get him down to the horse. And we're going to have to stand up to do it."

"Maybe not." She reached for the saddlebag. Opening the second side, she pulled out a small thermal blanket. "We can drag him."

"Do you have everything in that bag?"

"I was a Girl Scout."

He must have missed something. "A Girl Scout?"

"They teach you to be prepared. Always good, because around here, people are few and far between."

They spread the blanket and lifted Fahad onto it.

The canyon was quiet, nothing but the wind whistling through rock formations. Efraim would like to think that meant their shooter was gone, but he doubted that was the case.

Keeping low, Callie picked up one corner of the blanket near Fahad's head. Efraim took the other, and they slid him across rock to the three-foot drop down to the incline.

At the base of the steep slope, the palomino mare

stood, reins draped to the ground, shifting her hooves in the dust.

Efraim jumped off the rock shelf. His boots skidded on loose rock and debris. He went down to a knee before catching himself.

"You okay?" Callie said, her voice breathless.

He nodded. "I'll take him from here." He gathered Fahad in his arms as if cradling a baby. Fahad was only five feet eight inches tall, but he was built like a bulldog. A muscled bulldog at that. Efraim's arms ached with his limp weight. At least the sucking noise had stopped. His cousin's breathing was still labored, but he was breathing.

Efraim half skidded, half ran down the slope to the horse, Callie right behind him. The place she'd left the horses was protected on several sides. Except for the rock shelf above, most of the canyon plummeted downward from their perch, and afforded a decent view of the area. Not that there was anything to see.

And that made Efraim nervous.

He lowered Fahad to the ground and hunched down beside him.

"How is he?"

"He's breathing better but unconscious."

"The pain. The blood loss. It probably got to be too much."

An understatement. He'd never had a gunshot wound, not in all his years in the military. But years ago, he'd helped a soldier who'd been shot during an uprising in Nadar. He knew how painful it could be.

He squinted up at the sun in the western sky. They were running out of time, and there was still someone out there gunning for them. He had to figure out what to do next. And he couldn't afford to make another mistake. "This ranch of your family's, how far?"

"A few miles."

"Can we still make it before nightfall?"

"Maybe. Or just after." She glanced at Fahad. "We'll have to take things slow."

The sun beat down, hot on his skin. Sweat stung his eyes. He wiped the back of his hand across his brow, realizing too late he had blood up to his elbows. And now, no doubt, all over his face. "You take Fahad on the horse."

"And you?"

"I stay here. Cover you."

She shook her head, her hair blowing in the wind and lashing her cheeks like whips. "No. That's not going to happen."

"What, then? We have an injured man, one horse and someone trying to shoot us." He wished she had another answer, a better answer, but he doubted one existed.

"You take him. I cover you."

"*That* is not going to happen."

"But this shooter, if he's targeting you—"

"Targeting me? And what if he is? You're not law enforcement. I suppose you're planning to use diplomacy?"

She stepped to her horse and tapped the stock of her prize rifle for an answer, throwing his earlier gesture back at him.

"Shooting targets is one thing. Engaging an enemy is another."

"You thought I was good enough a few minutes ago."

He shook his head. He hated to break it to her, but a few minutes ago, she'd been relatively protected. The riskier job had been climbing up to help Fahad. "I'm sure you're a fine shot. But this isn't the same thing."

She blew a frustrated breath through pursed lips. "COIN can proceed without me. It will die without you."

So that was it. He should have known. The COIN summit was obviously more important to her than her own life. Good thing that wasn't true for him. "That's not the way it works, Callie."

"Is this some sort of macho thing?"

"It's some sort of practical thing. You said your family's ranch is the closest place to get help. I have no idea how to get there. I can, however, hold a gunman off and catch up with you once I know it's safe."

She pressed her lips into a line, her chin set.

He didn't know Callie McGuire very well, but he already knew that look.

She met his eyes. "We'll both go. Together."

"Then we'll both get killed. And Fahad will die from his injuries," he said in a low voice. He glanced at his cousin. Fahad's breathing was labored, but the slicker looked to have done the trick. For now. But with every second they spent arguing, he was getting weaker and the sun was dipping lower in the western sky. "If you want to keep Nadar in the COIN compact, we need to keep Fahad alive. His death will only give the dissenters in Nadar fuel for their movement."

"And *your* death?"

"I'm not going to die."

She shook her head.

"Fahad is losing blood with each minute we spend arguing."

"Okay, okay. I'll do this your way." Her eyes focused on him like blue lasers. "But you have to promise me you'll catch up. That you'll be okay."

The slight tremble in her voice held a desperation that made his breath hitch, and for a moment, he wanted to believe she was concerned about him, personally, not merely politics and business negotiations, but him as a man.

"Promise me," she repeated.

"I give you my word."

She scrambled to her feet. "Then help me get him on the horse."

Chapter Three

This whole thing was wrong. All wrong.

Callie swung onto Sasha's back. When she'd ridden out to Rattlesnake Badlands at Prince Stefan's request, she'd been aiming to talk Efraim into going back to the resort where he'd be safe. Instead, he was risking his life for his cousin's, for hers. And unless she was willing to let Fahad die, she couldn't do a damn thing to change it.

"Fahad," Efraim said, kneeling next to his cousin. "Can you hear me?"

Fahad mumbled something Callie couldn't quite catch. His eyes fluttered and opened. His face twisted in a grimace of pain.

"I am going to lift you onto the horse. It might get a bit rough. Hang with us, okay?"

Fahad just kept breathing, in and out, as if anything else was beyond his grasp. It probably was.

Efraim glanced up at her. "Ready?"

She wasn't sure how they were going to pull this off. Fahad couldn't lie on his back across the saddle. Nor could he drape over it on his belly, letting blood rush to his head. She slipped behind the saddle's cantle and sat on the stiff, leather skirt. "He's going to have to sit on the seat. That's the only way this is going to work." Even then, she wasn't sure they could manage.

Efraim knelt down. Fitting his hands under Fahad's shoulders and knees, he lifted the man from the ground and climbed to his feet.

Callie reached down from the saddle, and Efraim hoisted him onto the seat. Callie guided his leg over the saddle until he sat astride. She settled him on the seat and leaned his body back against her. She could feel him groan, the sound shuddering through her body. She steadied him with one hand and held Sasha's reins with the other.

"Do you have him?"

Good question. With a man who had the strength of a rag doll sitting on her lap and her legs dangling at her mare's flanks, Callie had a challenge ahead of her. She was grateful the horse was Sasha. The palomino mare could read Callie's shifts of weight almost as if she was reading her mind.

She looked down at Efraim. The thought of him out facing the man who did this to Fahad chilled her to the core. If only she could do something.

He had his pistol, but a pistol wasn't going to do much good unless the shooter was close. Balancing Fahad against her chest, she tapped the stock of her rifle. "Take this."

He shook his head. "You'll need it."

"Between balancing Fahad on the saddle and keeping control of Sasha, I don't have enough hands to use a rifle. Give me your pistol."

He unbuckled his holster. Reaching up, he helped

her strap it around her waist. She pulled the rifle from its scabbard and handed it to him.

His hand closed around hers. He lingered for a moment, then took the rifle. "Go."

She clucked to Sasha and the horse moved forward. Callie kept her eyes on the horizon in the direction of the Seven M Ranch, resisting the need to look around, to see Efraim taking cover among the hoodoos and cliffs, to watch as he faded into the distance.

Two gunshots cracked and echoed off the rock.

Callie kept Sasha moving forward. She knew the shots were likely Efraim drawing attention to himself, trying to let her ride away unnoticed. She forced herself not to think of what might happen next, but her imagination niggled around the edges anyway. Efraim shot... Efraim lying in Rattlesnake Badlands alone while the life drained from his body... Efraim sacrificing himself to make sure she could escape.

A sob stuck in her throat.

In all the times she'd spoken to him before today, she'd had to remind herself to be professional. Speak about COIN and the future of Nadar. Don't get too personal. Don't hold his gaze too long.

She'd been attracted to him from the first time she'd laid eyes on him, at a reception in Kyros, his hair nearly as black as his tuxedo. Each time she'd spoken with him since, she'd felt on the edge of giggling and blushing. She'd had to force herself to remain professional.

And now?

Now she just wanted to talk to him again. She just wanted to look in his eyes and feel that blush one more time.

Sasha cleared the badlands. The landscape flattened into sage-pocked plains and abrupt, flat-topped hills called benches. The mountains loomed closer on the northern horizon. The scent of pine tickled the dry wind.

The going was slow, even on the more even ground. With each sway of Sasha's stride, Callie could feel Fahad's weight tip to one side or the other as he grew weaker and even less able to hold himself steady. He was a big man. Not as tall as Efraim, but thick and muscled. If he tilted too far to either side, she wouldn't be able to hold him.

The sun dipped lower in the western sky, its aurora kissing the blue shadow of mountains before starting its slip behind. Soon she would have to navigate by the glow of twilight. She needed to keep moving. Among the mountains, twilight seemed to last forever. But when night finally fell, it was blacker than a nightmare.

"Efraim." Fahad's voice was low, a harsh whisper.

Callie leaned her face close to his. The rusty scent of blood filled each breath she took. "He'll catch up with us. He'll be okay."

"You let him…"

She finished the rest of his sentence with her imagination. An extra shard of guilt dug into her. "I didn't let him. He insisted on protecting you, protecting me."

"You care only for your negotiations."

His words hit her like a slap. "That's not true." She'd been telling herself that that was all she *should* care about ever since she'd first met Efraim. That she should be professional. That she should think only of her job. Now a part of her wished she'd never listened.

"He shouldn't die…"

His voice was growing weak. She leaned closer.

"…you should."

"I should what?"

"Die."

The vitriol in his one word shook her to the core. She'd faced opposition before in her job. Hatred for the United States. Distrust. She'd faced some of the same from the people she'd grown up with. But never had someone wished her death straight to her face. "I'm sorry you feel that way."

"You have polluted Efraim."

"Polluted?" Words gathered in her mind, bitter words she longed to throw back. She bit the inside of her lip. Pouring gasoline on this kind of fire would only make it burn brighter, hotter. She would let him have his say.

"You, your country…let him go."

Let him go? "Efraim does what he feels is best. I have no hold on him."

"Let him go."

All her experience as a diplomat, and she had no idea what to say to the man. She could find no words. "Efraim makes his own choices."

"Then may you both…" A rasping sound vibrated through his chest and back. He strained backward, against Callie, as if struggling to breathe.

She shifted him to the side.

"Your family and his…may both be destroyed." He slumped heavily against her. He gasped in a labored breath, then another.

She grasped the saddle's fork and held on.

"Whoa, Sasha." Reaching around the other side of him, she transferred the reins into the hand gripping the saddle. She threaded her free hand along the man's neck and felt for his pulse. His skin felt clammy. Sweat soaked his hair, his beard. A faint, thready rhythm beat against her fingers.

Still alive, but for how long?

She picked up the reins again and clucked to Sasha. Eyes on the horizon, she searched for the telltale signs of the creek that wound through her family's ranch while the sun slipped behind the mountain range.

EFRAIM HELD HIS GUN at the ready and strode toward the flash of movement he'd seen between clumps of sage. Probably an animal. A pronghorn antelope darting across the land or a coyote scrounging for food or scampering after a rodent. But deep down he feared it wasn't something so innocuous. Whoever had shot Fahad was still out here. Watching him. Following. He sensed him.

At least he hoped the gunman was following him and not Callie and Fahad.

He could no longer see them. He hadn't been able to for quite a while now, even over this open stretch. But he could see her horse's fresh tracks among sagebrush and prickly pear. And at his pace, he had to be closing in on her. Of course, with only the faint glow of the sun from beyond the mountains, seeing anything was becoming a challenge.

A slight rustle carried on the dying wind.

Ahead, vegetation grew a little taller, a little more lush. A clear indication of water. Probably a creek. He pulled out Callie's rifle. Lifting it to his shoulder, he peered through the scope and scanned the area.

No horse. No man. But also no animal. At least not one he could see.

Whoever was out there was very good. Either someone who knew the land, or someone trained to disappear. He could be lining Efraim up in his sights right now, and Efraim wouldn't even know he was there.

Not until the bullet hit.

He tried to clear his mind, to focus on what his senses told him, not what his imagination could invent. Whoever was out there had been following Callie or him or both since Fahad was shot. He hadn't shot back since his second attempt in the badlands, but that didn't mean killing them wasn't his aim. Efraim just wished he knew why the man was playing with them like a cat plays with its prey before devouring it.

Dry soil crunched under his boots. The wind had died down with the fall of night, and the air was still, making every sound loud as gunfire. He breathed deeply, searching for the scent of burning tobacco, the sharp tang of a man's sweat, something, but all he could detect was the ever-present fragrance of sage flavored with a distant hint of pine.

He lowered the rifle. Another thing he hadn't seen was any sign of a ranch, and that had him worried. It couldn't be too much farther, could it? He hoped it was as close as Callie thought. And he could only pray Fahad was still alive and strong enough for it to matter.

The hiss sounded from the prairie floor, like the shake of a maraca, louder than the wind.

Oh, hell.

He looked down at the earth in front of him.

The black coil of a rattlesnake lay near a clump of sage. Again, it sounded its deadly warning.

Efraim took a slow step backward. Then another. In all the riding and climbing he'd done in Rattlesnake Badlands, he hadn't seen a single one of the reptiles. They'd probably been hiding from the hot sun. This one had ventured out to enjoy the cooler evening air.

He took several more backward steps.

The rattle faltered, then stopped. He'd barely drawn a breath when another sound came from behind him. The unmistakable clack of a rifle chambering a round.

"Turn around and I'll blow your head off."

The voice sounded American. A local, or at least a pretty good imitation of the accent. A slight tremor vibrated under the words.

Efraim gripped the rifle. He slid his finger to the trigger guard.

"Throw the rifle down."

Could he spin around, aim and fire before the man could take him out? He doubted it. He'd proven himself quite a marksman in the canyon. Now, with what sounded like only a few yards between them, hitting Efraim would be child's play.

"I said throw it down."

It would be smarter to wait for a better chance. He just prayed it would come before the bullet did. He tossed Callie's rifle to the ground.

"Put your hands up."

Efraim complied. Hands raised, he scanned the area, straining to see in the dim light. Sagebrush hulked in low, gray mounds, but he could see little else. Nothing he could use for cover.

Boots crunched on dry ground. The steps came closer, moving up behind him.

Efraim held his breath. He could feel the man closing in. Only eight feet away. Four. Two. Efraim no longer had his pistol or Callie's rifle, but that didn't mean he was unarmed. He slowed his breathing, focused his mind, ready to move.

The footfalls stopped. Efraim could sense him bend down, hear him grab Callie's rifle.

Now.

Efraim slashed a hand downward, grabbing for his belt. The dagger decorating the buckle looked like simple ornamentation, but it was anything but. His thumb found the release button at the same time his fingers hit the tiny dagger. He pulled the small blade clear and spun around.

The man was a dark silhouette, the last glow of twilight behind him.

Efraim slashed, hit flesh.

The man let loose a guttural sound.

Efraim reversed direction, bringing the blade back, striking again.

This time his enemy was ready. He lifted the rifle. Blade hit barrel.

The dagger wrenched from Efraim's hands. The rifle barrel numbed his hand and plowed into his side.

Pain shot through his ribcage, making it hard to breathe. He struck out with his bare hands. His knuckles glanced off the man's chin.

The rifle hit again.

His whole chest seized with pain. Gasping, Efraim hunched forward, trying to protect his ribs, trying to breathe.

The man was on him in a second. His knee drove into Efraim's back. Dirt and grit ground into his cheek. He struggled for air but nothing came.

"Hold still."

Efraim finally choked a breath into his lungs. Dust came with it. He coughed, his side on fire. The entire middle of his body wreathed in pain.

His dagger.

It had flown out of his hand when the rifle barrel hit. It had to be here. Within a few feet. He scraped the ground in front of him with his free hand, but hit nothing but sagebrush and prickly pear.

"Hold still." The man shoved his knee harder into Efraim's back. "Right now, or I'll blow you away."

Each inhale seared like a hot poker in the side, but at least he was breathing. He felt something hard press into the back of his head.

"Is he dead?"

"Who?" Efraim managed to choke out.

"The one I shot."

Efraim dug his fingers into the dirt. He didn't know if Fahad was alive or dead, but either way he would strangle the man with his own hands. He would avenge his cousin. His blood. Fahad would do no less for him.

"Is he?"

"No."

He let out a breath with a whoosh. "Why are you here?" The man's voice cracked.

Efraim smiled. It was one thing to gun a man down

from a distance. Looking through a rifle scope made everything seem unreal, like watching a violent movie or playing a video game. Americans loved their violence as long as it was at a distance. Pretend. Or in someone else's country.

Efraim knew how to deal with it close up.

He had to be calm, to clear his mind. He'd struck too fast with the knife. Played it too recklessly. He'd assumed he was faster than his enemy. As fast as he had been years ago when he'd fought for Nadar. He'd been wrong. But he didn't need to be faster. He was smarter. This time he needed to think. And when he got an opening, he needed to make it count.

The guy had him pinned to the ground, but his weight rested too much on Efraim's back. In that unstable position, Efraim could throw him off balance and flip him. He'd already proven himself more fond of throwing threats around than bullets. He'd give Efraim another chance. Cracked rib or not, Efraim could take him. He tensed, ready to make his move.

"Efraim?"

Callie.

Bloody hell. She must be near. She must have heard voices. And knowing what he did of her, she was probably on her way to help.

Efraim could feel the man tense at the sound of her voice. He still had his rifle, probably two, because he'd taken Callie's, as well. Maybe that was what he was waiting for…for all three of them to be together. Maybe he was following, being as quiet as he could, biding his time so he could take them all out at the same time.

"Efraim? Is that you?"

She was closer. Riding straight into his trap. Straight toward a man with a gun.

Efraim couldn't let Callie be his target. "Callie? Run." He bucked backward, trying to unseat the man.

The man was too quick. He shifted his weight off Efraim and brought his fist hard into Efraim's side.

Into his cracked rib.

Pain ripped through his body. A gasp tore from his lips. For a second, he couldn't move.

Gritting his teeth, he forced his body to function. He sprang upward and back, but the man was off him and he connected with nothing but air.

A shadow moved to the left.

He spun to the side with a kick. This time he hit flesh.

The man grunted but kept moving. Running. Not toward Efraim or the sound of Callie's voice but away. Footsteps ground on dry earth and faded into the night.

Efraim tried to run, to give chase, but after a few steps, he knew it was no good. He slumped forward, bracing his hands on his knees. Pain tore through his side, making each breath agony. Cracked rib for certain. Maybe two. He forced himself to straighten, took a few steps in the direction the shooter went, then doubled over again.

"Efraim? Are you okay?"

He turned toward her voice. All he could make out was the silhouette of a horse carrying two riders. She was near him, only a few feet away. But he couldn't see her face.

"Efraim?"

"I'm fine," he lied.

"I heard voices. Fighting. What happened?" Her voice trembled, frightened for him, not sparing a thought about what she was rushing into.

At once he felt grateful for her concern and angry that she'd exposed herself to such danger. "You should have run for the ranch. You shouldn't have risked coming back for me."

"And let you die?"

"I wasn't going to die." He was close enough to see her face now, her golden hair. But he couldn't read her eyes. But there was something, the sheen of tears on her cheeks... "Callie? You're crying. What happened?"

Her breath hitched. "I'm so sorry, I—I think Fahad is dead."

Chapter Four

Efraim didn't want to believe Callie's words, but somehow he knew they were true. He stumbled forward, reaching the horse's side.

"His pulse, I checked. The first time, it felt weak. But this last time...I couldn't find it at all."

Fahad was slumped to the side, Callie gripping the fork of the saddle, stretching her arm like a gate to keep him from falling off. Efraim had to wonder how long she'd been riding like that.

"Do you want to check? I mean, to make sure?"

He glanced around. Sagebrush dotted the ground around them, darker hulks in a dark world. The gunman could be anywhere. Twenty feet away, and they might not be able to see him. "We need to get out of here. Can you hold Fahad upright a little longer?"

"I think so."

He had a feeling she would, no matter how numb her arm became, no matter how slick the saddle leather felt under her fingers. He had to hurry.

Again he scanned the darkness. The fight had thrown off his sense of direction. With the clouds low and no sign of the sun's glow behind the mountains, he couldn't get his bearings. "Which way?"

"To your right."

He turned the way she'd suggested.

"See the big sage and Russian olive? That's the creek that runs through my family's ranch. We can follow it right to the Seven M."

He took the palomino mare's reins and started leading her toward the larger shadows. He pulled in short breaths, pain shooting through his side. He struggled to listen, to hear the rustle of human boots moving through the sparse vegetation. But the only sounds that reached him were the four-beat rhythm of the horse's walk and the faint creak of the broken-in saddle. After a while, he added the gurgle of the creek to his list. In the distance, a dog barked.

"You hear that?" Callie asked. "The dog. That's my dad's border collie."

So they were getting close. Not that it mattered for Fahad. But at least Callie would be safe.

Fahad. Dead.

He still couldn't believe it, couldn't accept it. "Try to find his pulse again."

Callie shifted in the saddle and the horse stopped. She brought her hand to Fahad's neck. Seconds passed. She met Efraim's gaze and shook her head. "You check."

He reached up. Callie took his hand and guided it to Fahad's throat. As soon as Efraim touched his skin, he knew. It felt cool, much cooler than it should. He didn't have to search for a pulse, but he did anyway.

A weight bore down on his chest. His throat thickened as if filled with sand. He'd thought the pain of a broken rib was bad. This was much worse. He tried to swallow, to take a breath, but he couldn't.

Fahad had told him leaving the ranch was dangerous. He hadn't listened. He hadn't cared about the danger to himself. It had never occurred to him the danger would be to Fahad. And now to Callie McGuire, as well.

Efraim wasn't a devout Muslim, but he wished he were more devout now. Maybe then he'd know what prayers to offer for his cousin's soul. Maybe then he could breathe. Maybe then he'd know how to feel.

He looked up at Callie, bravely holding on, cradling Fahad's body, even though she had known for quite some time that he was dead. She'd done it for him, Efraim knew. To give them time to get closer to the ranch and away from the gunman. But even more, to give him time to accept that his cousin was, indeed, gone. "Release your grip."

Even in the dark, he could sense her searching his eyes. "Are you sure?" she asked.

He nodded. "You've done enough. I will take him."

She let go. Fahad slumped to the side and into Efraim's arms. He held his cousin's body while Callie slid to the ground, shaking the blood back into her arm. He was heavy, but Efraim could only half feel the weight. The knowledge that he wouldn't have died if not for Efraim's actions weighed far heavier.

His legs faltered.

Suddenly Callie was beside him, her hand on his arm, her voice in his ear. "Put him down."

Efraim staggered. He dropped to one knee. The darkness around him blurred. The pain in his side grew and spread until it swallowed all of him. He lay Fahad on the ground and let a shudder take him. Another followed and another. "It's my fault," he managed to choke out.

"No." Callie brought her hand to his cheek. She wiped his face, then turned him to face her.

He knew she wanted to say something, but he didn't want to hear it. He didn't want to think. He didn't want to feel. At least not what he was feeling now.

She looked so soft, so beautiful, so caring. Even in the darkness, her eyes sparkled like the clearest water. Her hair draped over her shoulders like a veil.

He pulled her to him, cupped his hand around the nape of her neck, brought his lips to hers. She tasted sweet, yet salty, her tears mixing with his own. Tears shed for him, he knew. And for Fahad, whom she'd hardly even met.

He knew he shouldn't be kissing her. And yet he needed this. At this moment, he felt like he couldn't do without it.

She was something, this woman. Strong and determined, yet with a tender heart. What he wouldn't give to stay in her arms, to make her his. To wake every day to a woman like this. To let her be his reason for living.

An impossible dream.

Efraim ended the kiss and looked down. He knew he should feel ashamed. How could he kiss a woman over his cousin's dead body? How could he claim warm feelings for himself when his actions had sentenced Fahad to his death? Yet although he accepted the blame for Fahad following him to the badlands, he couldn't manage to regret kissing Callie. That he kept for himself.

She took his hands in hers. "Don't blame yourself."

He looked up at the sound of her voice and found

her watching him. It was all he could do to keep from kissing her again. "How can I not?"

"It was his job to protect you."

"And I made him follow me because I refused to listen. I never thought, never considered I was risking others' lives, not just my own."

"You had your reasons for riding to Rattlesnake Badlands. Reasons that weren't selfish. And Fahad did his job. He tried to make sure you were safe. The man who shot him, he deserves the blame."

He nodded and gave her fingers a squeeze. Fahad had fulfilled his responsibility to Efraim. It was now Efraim's turn. "You are right."

"We'll tie him on Sasha. We'll take him to my family's ranch and call the sheriff. He will find whoever did this and make him pay."

"No."

She lowered her brows and tilted her head, as if she wasn't following.

"Fahad is my family, my blood, not the sheriff's."

She frowned, a crease digging between her eyebrows. "You have to leave this to the law, Efraim."

He let out a derisive laugh he could feel shoot down his side. "The law can't avenge Fahad. I can."

"That's not the way things work here."

"As far as I can see, things don't work here very well. Otherwise Amir would not be gone. Stefan would not have been attacked. Fahad would not be dead."

"You're upset. You just lost your cousin. It's understandable. But we are a nation of laws and the law works. It does." She nodded as if she could will him to agree.

"Sheriff Wolf is a good man, an honest man. He'll give Fahad justice."

He wasn't upset. He wasn't angry. He merely felt cold. Resolute. He looked away from her, not wanting to see what was in her eyes, not wanting to have his resolve shaken. It would be so easy to be tempted to selfishly forget Fahad, forget what he owed his security man, his cousin, his blood, and instead lose himself in the woman in front of him.

The spark of a light caught his eye.

He climbed to his feet, Callie rising beside him. The light moved in their direction. In the stillness, he could hear horses' hooves clatter across rocky terrain, buckles jingling, leather creaking. "Give me the Glock." He held out his hand.

"It's my family. They're looking for me."

"How do you know?"

"I know."

He wasn't sure he was prepared to trust she was right. "Give it to me anyway."

Her eyebrows dipped low. She shook her head.

He wasn't sure if she thought he was going to take his measure of justice from her family or what. After all he'd said, he guessed he couldn't blame her. "They'll help?"

"Of course they'll help. We'll go to the ranch. We can call the sheriff from there."

He still wasn't convinced he trusted her plan, but he probably didn't need to point that out to Callie again. "Fine."

The sounds drew closer. The light wound along the creek toward them. It focused upward, pinning them in its beam. Efraim couldn't see a thing except blinding white light. Hoofbeats spread in a circle around them.

Efraim squinted against the glare. Blue splotches bloomed wherever he looked, like twenty spotlights bearing down. One man held the light. The others were merely dark. Efraim focused on the ground, trying to see the men around him in his peripheral vision. There were three, no, four mounted men. He glanced at Callie.

"Put your hands up where I can see them." The voice boomed from behind the spotlight, the accent no-nonsense Wyoming rancher.

Efraim raised his hands.

"Now on your knees."

Efraim shook his head. Had Callie been wrong? Was this her family, or some kind of vigilante mob like the one Stefan said had been protesting in Dumont? "I'm Efraim Aziz. I—"

Rounds slid into rifle chambers. "I said on your knees."

CALLIE COULDN'T believe it. She glanced around the circle of shadows on horseback. Never in a million years would she imagine her family drawing down on her. She'd told Efraim all these pie-in-the-sky things about justice in America, and here her own family seemed to be taking the law into their own hands. She wanted to hang her head in shame. "Daddy, put the gun down. Brent? Russ? Timmy?" she said, taking a guess at which brothers had accompanied her father.

"Move behind us, Callie."

"Behind you?" Now she was getting angry. "What are you? Thick? Efraim and I, we're together."

One of her brothers sputtered out a cough.

"Callie, you don't understand what's going on here," her father said in a gruff voice. "Move behind your brothers."

Callie didn't move from Efraim's side. "I understand perfectly what's going on. My family is causing an international incident. *That's* what's going on."

The light her father was shining on Efraim flicked down to the ground, highlighting Fahad's still body. "Who is that man?"

"Fahad Bahir," Efraim said. "My head security man. My cousin."

"He dead?"

"Shot," Efraim said. "Murdered."

Callie's stomach tightened at the dark tone in his voice. His words about vengeance scuttled through the back of her mind. Between Efraim's anger and her family's obvious defensiveness, this situation could get bad fast. She couldn't let things spin out of control. "He was wounded. We were trying to get him back to the ranch, but he died on the way. We have to call the sheriff."

"How'd he get shot?"

"A sniper in Rattlesnake Badlands."

"The question is, why did he get shot? What was he doing?" Brent's voice.

Already tight, Callie's stomach dropped. Her oldest brother had done four tours in Afghanistan until a head injury ended his military career. Since then he'd had a hard time of it. Seizures. Paranoia. Trying to get used to returning to life on the ranch, a life he hadn't much cared for.

Callie felt bad for him. She would feel worse, except

that every horror he'd seen and every hardship he lived through, he blamed squarely on any person of Middle Eastern descent who crossed his path. Luckily in Wyoming, there weren't a lot of people on which to focus his anger over what had happened to him.

Until now.

"Mr. Bahir was protecting Sheik Efraim."

"Protecting him from what?"

Efraim had to hear the sneer in her brother's voice. Callie just prayed he didn't lash back.

"There are people who want me and my people dead." Efraim's voice was steady.

Callie gave him a grateful look she hoped he could read despite the glaring light.

"I'll bet there are lots of people who want you and yours dead. And I'll bet you've done a few things to them to cause it."

Callie swung a much less charitable glare on her brother. "Brent, stop it."

"One of these people shot Fahad. He followed us from the badlands and attacked me."

"And what were you doing wandering around those badlands?"

"Searching for a friend."

"On foot? How did you get out there?"

"My horse ran. He was afraid of gunfire."

"That horse—" Joe's voice. At least one of her sane brothers was on this trip. A schoolteacher, husband and new father, Joe helped out on the ranch in the summer and some weekends. Apparently he'd stopped by today after Callie had ridden out.

"We need to get to the ranch, Dad," Callie repeated,

feeling a bit bolstered by Joe's presence and Efraim's continued calm. "We need to call the sheriff."

"How do we know he isn't going to try to pull something?" Russ's voice. Second to youngest in age, Russ idolized Brent, even planning to go into military service himself after he got his degree and could enter as an officer. His plans had changed after Brent's injury.

Unlike his big brother, Russ had always taken to ranch work. Callie's father called Russ his natural cowboy. Unfortunately his unshakable hero worship of Brent caused him to absorb everything his oldest brother said like a sponge. He tended to follow Brent's lead in all things, unless Callie could get to him first.

Unfortunately her job had her traveling all over the world, and she hadn't been able to spend much time on the ranch the last couple of years. She had the feeling that this time she might be too late to influence Russ. "He's with me, Russ."

"That better not mean what I think it means," Brent grumbled.

Callie's cheeks heated as the sensations of her kiss with Efraim flitted through the back of her mind.

"Callie is working with me through her office."

Efraim again. He'd just lost his cousin, one of the closest men in his administration, not to mention his friend going missing, and yet he was steadier and calmer than the men in her family. Men who before this, she would have sworn were steady and calm.

"Her office, yeah. Foreign Affairs," Russ drawled out, putting emphasis on the word *affairs*.

"Grow up, Russell," she snapped. For a boy almost

out of college, he was more immature than their high school–aged youngest brother.

"What do you mean, grow up? I'm not the one messing around with a damn Arab. Hell, he's probably a terrorist."

She blew a frustrated stream of air through tight lips and focused on her father. She wished she could peer past the light and see his eyes. Better yet, she wished her father would stop shining the damn thing on Efraim like he was a subject in some kind of interrogation. "Efraim is one of the good guys. The leader of a country."

"A country that is an enemy of the United States?"

Brent again. It seemed like she'd spent most of her life smoothing things over between her big brother and the rest of the world. Callie wanted to belt him. "Efraim is not an enemy. He's not a terrorist. Get it? He's the leader of a country named Nadar, and he's here to negotiate a contract brokered by the United States." Her voice shook with the effort to keep it even when she really wanted to scream.

They answered her with silence. The spotlight still glared in Efraim's eyes.

"Please, Daddy. Why would I tell you something that's not true?"

Her father didn't answer, but Russ did. "Because you're hot for him. Don't lie, sis. You're pretty obvious."

She closed her eyes. Of course, Russ was closer than she wanted to admit. At least she should be grateful the spotlight's beam prevented Efraim from seeing her blush.

"Admit it," Russ continued, clearly encouraged by hitting on the truth. "You're covering for him."

"I don't need to cover for him. He hasn't done anything wrong."

Her father flashed the light back down to the ground for a second. "Someone killed this man."

"Fahad is my blood. My head security man. I didn't kill him."

"The person who did tried to kill Efraim, too," Callie added quickly. "That someone is still out there. We need to get to the ranch. We need to make sure Efraim's safe."

"I'm more concerned about you."

Of course he was. He was her dad after all. And maybe she could use that fact to break this stalemate. "Then get *me* to the ranch. And call the sheriff."

"You," he said, bobbing the light to indicate Efraim. "Pick up that body. Throw him on the horse we caught."

"The horse you caught?" Callie hadn't noticed the horse behind Russ, but as her brother led it into the spotlight, she recognized Efraim's gelding.

"You found him."

"Him?" Russ tilted his head.

"The horse. It's Efraim's." She'd told Efraim the horse would find his way to safety. She was relieved to be proven right.

Efraim lifted Fahad. Joe dismounted and helped Efraim slump the dead man over the saddle. Using his lariat, Joe tied him securely.

"Good to go," Brent said to his father, and Joe swung back on his horse.

"You," her father barked, obviously meaning Efraim.

"Walk ahead. And remember we got rifles pointed at your back."

"Daddy—"

He held up a hand, blocking her complaint. "I'm doing the rest of what you asked, Callie. I trust you, honey, but that doesn't mean I trust this boy."

Efraim glanced back at her. "It's all right."

It wasn't all right. Her family was behaving horribly. She'd told him they would help, and technically, she supposed, they were. But she didn't know if Efraim would see it that way. She felt she needed to apologize.

She just hoped that after all this, he'd give her the chance.

Her father nodded, as if it was settled, and motioned to Brent and Joe. "The two of you keep looking. Russ and I will see Callie and the sheik here back to the ranch."

"Looking?" A frisson of fear fanned over Callie's skin. The thought of her brothers out on the dark BLM searching for a murderer scared the breath out of her. "Don't be ridiculous. We need to call the sheriff. He can look for the man who shot Fahad. It's his job. Not yours."

"We're not looking for some terrorist killer," Brent said. "We're looking for Timmy's ATV."

"Timmy's ATV?" Callie had been so wrapped up in defending Efraim, she hadn't thought there might be a reason her fourth brother, the youngest in the family at only seventeen, wasn't riding with them. "Why? What happened? Where's Timmy?"

"Timmy's home. He crashed his ATV."

"Is he okay?" The thought of her baby brother hurt... She wanted to race Sasha home as fast as she could.

"He's banged up. A little worse for wear," Joe said. "But you know Timmy. He'll be okay."

"What happened to his ATV?"

"He flipped the damn thing." Her dad lowered the light enough for her to see him shaking his head. Then he brought the beam back to Efraim's face. "Wasn't Tim's fault, though. He said someone shot out a tire."

Chapter Five

If Efraim had thought Callie's family interrogating him like he was some kind of criminal was humiliating, this was worse. He marched in front of the group of horsemen, guns pointed at his back as if he was a prisoner.

He supposed he was.

At least he could see where he was walking. Spotlight shining on his back instead of his face, the land in front of him was lit nearly as bright as day, save for his long shadow stretching across sage and rock and the ruts of a dirt utility road.

The long trudge gave him some time to think. His mind was still reeling from Fahad's death. If only he had listened and not gone out on his own searching for signs of Amir. Fahad's death was his fault. Pure and simple. And it was up to him to make sure the man who killed his cousin paid the price.

And then there was Callie. Before today, he'd been powerfully attracted to her. Kissing her had brought a flood of emotion for which he wasn't prepared. The feelings she'd awakened swirled and mixed with his guilt and grief and anger until he couldn't sort one from the other. He needed to get some distance from her, from all of this. Sort things out. He needed to do what was right for his country, for Fahad's memory, for himself. Most of all, he had to get back to the resort, regroup and figure out what to do next.

The McGuire ranch seemed to encompass more square miles than Nadar's capital city. Efraim didn't know how many head of cattle the McGuires ran, but judging from the herds he saw, it was an impressive number. Wire fence glistened in the spotlight's glare, stretching for what looked like forever. Finally they could see the lighted ranch yard. The hulking shape of a barn came into view followed by the outline of a white clapboard house the size of a small hotel. They followed the dirt tracks. Lights shone down from two utility poles and illuminated the yard.

Callie's father switched off his spotlight. He circled Efraim on a tall, chestnut gelding and stopped in front of him. "Russ?"

Callie's brother gathered all the horses' reins in one hand and braced his rifle on the fork of his saddle, covering Efraim. "Got him."

Callie's father dismounted and took over the vigil.

"Dad, this is ridiculous," Callie said, for what seemed like the hundredth time. "Sheik Efraim is a foreign dignitary. He did not shoot out the tires on Timmy's ATV."

"Callie, hitch Sasha to the post."

Callie didn't move. "He was also with me."

"Really? How long was he with you? Every moment?"

Callie didn't answer.

"Just as I thought."

"Dad, a man has been murdered."

"And we're lucky your brother wasn't murdered, too."

"We need to call the sheriff," she prodded. "And Sheik Efraim's people at the Wind River Ranch."

"We will." Her father's tone softened, giving in. He offered his daughter a nod. "But we'll do it in the house…where the phone is, all right?"

Callie glanced at Efraim and pressed her lips together in a grim smile. "The sheriff, he'll find Fahad's murderer. I promise."

How she could promise something over which she had no control, he couldn't understand, but he returned her press of the lips just the same.

"Russ," Callie's father said, turning to the remaining brother. "Put up the horses."

Russ put his own rifle away and gathered the reins from his father, a horse on either side of his own. "What do you want me to do with the dead guy?"

A wave of emotion swept over Efraim. He closed his eyes against it.

He felt closer to Fahad than to his own brother or to his sisters whom he barely knew. Losing Fahad was more than losing his security man; it was like losing a leg, a part of him. And he had no close family, no strong beliefs, nothing to use as a crutch.

"Tie the horse in a stall," Callie's father directed. "Just leave him on the saddle. We'll let the sheriff deal with him."

Deal with him. Hours tied to a horse. Then being shunted off on a gurney. Poking and prodding. An autopsy.

Efraim tried to block thoughts of the indignities to Fahad's remains that would doubtlessly follow. There was little he could do to restore his cousin's dignity until he learned who his murder was. Only then could he right a small portion of the wrong.

The McGuire home was surprisingly warm and inviting inside. He would never guess that it was the home of men. In one of the few times Callie and he had talked, she'd mentioned her mother's death. No doubt she had been quite a woman, just like her only daughter. Even though she was now gone, Efraim could see her mark on everything from the flower beds outside to the cheery yellow wall color inside. While Callie made phone calls, he sat at a large kitchen table made of sturdy oak, drank glass after glass of cold water and waited for the sheriff to arrive.

The sheriff was nothing like what he expected. During his wait, he'd gotten a look at Callie's father and brother Russ in the bright kitchen light. They looked very much like Callie. Freckled, blond, maybe a hint of red in Russ's hair, average height, average build, what he thought of as the average American. He'd expected the same from the sheriff.

He'd been wrong.

With the black hair, black eyes and dark skin, Jake Wolf resembled no one in the McGuire house as much as Efraim himself. Obviously he wasn't of Middle Eastern descent, but Native American. However, Efraim had to admit the resemblance in coloring made him feel a little more at ease. A little less the enemy.

Efraim stood, his chair skidding backward, screeching on the floor. "Sheriff, I'm glad you're here."

Callie's father invited the sheriff into the kitchen with a wave of his arm. "Take a load off, Jake. Want some coffee?"

The sheriff held up a hand. "Thanks anyway, Clay. I'm good."

Efraim suppressed a groan. So much for fantasizing that he had an ally. Apparently the sheriff and Callie's father were on a first name basis. He couldn't fool himself into thinking his version of events would be considered as seriously as Clay McGuire's.

"Suit yourself. Like I told you on the phone, Mr. Aziz here knows the dead man."

"He's my head of security, my countryman and my cousin. His name is Fahad Bahir."

The sheriff flipped open a notebook and scribbled down the name. "Were you with him when he was shot?"

"We heard the gunshots and found him afterward." He told the sheriff how he'd ridden into the badlands, how Fahad had followed without his knowledge to protect him and how Callie had found him shortly before the first shot was fired.

"You and Callie were together when this happened?"

"Yes."

Callie's father gave a low grunt, as if he didn't believe any of it. Or maybe he just didn't like the idea of his daughter and Efraim in the same…world.

"After my horse broke free, we decided it would be best if Callie took Fahad and rode for her family's ranch."

"And you?"

"I stayed behind to face the gunman, to make sure he didn't follow."

"So the two of you weren't together the entire time." Clay McGuire nodded as if that was as good as if Efraim had admitted to shooting the tires of his son's vehicle. "You weren't together but for a little while, were you?"

The sheriff hooked a thumb in his wide leather belt. The howling wolf on the large silver buckle reminded Efraim of his own belt and the dagger which was lying somewhere among the sagebrush.

"Clay," the sheriff said. "I need to have a word with Callie and Mr. Aziz here about this murder. Alone. After that, you and I will have a chat with Timmy, add things up."

"All right, Jake."

Sheriff Wolf focused on Callie. "Is there someplace we can talk in private?"

"My father's study?" She glanced at her father, and he gave her a nod. "This way," she said.

They followed her down the hall and into a large room furnished in heavy wood and leather. A cross between an office and a personal retreat, the place was equipped with everything from computer and filing system to a large television and leather recliners. In addition to photos of rodeo action, the dark paneled walls were covered in the heads and horns of various large game.

Sheriff Wolf motioned for Efraim and Callie to sit in the leather chairs. Callie collapsed into the closest. Efraim remained standing.

"Tell me what happened," the sheriff said.

Between the two of them, they explained the events of the past hours in more detail, including the attack on Efraim and the injury to his ribs. Efraim watched Wolf's eyes, but try as he might to guess the sheriff's thoughts, he could read nothing.

A reason to be nervous right there.

When they finished, Wolf focused on Efraim. "What kind of business brings you and your countrymen to Wind River County?"

Of all questions Efraim expected the sheriff to ask, that wasn't on the list. It was also something he couldn't answer. Not in any detail. The COIN agreement was secret, and until the agreement was negotiated and signed, it had to remain so. Too much was at stake and too many special interests wanted to kill the compact. Or just cut off a nice piece of it for themselves.

Besides, after all Stefan had gone through, he didn't trust local law enforcement. None of the COIN leaders did.

Nor had Fahad.

"You don't need to know about that," Efraim said.

"A man has been murdered. His death might be tied to all that has been going on in my county the past few days—since, may I add, you and your friends at the Wind River Ranch and Resort rolled into town. I need to know every detail."

"I'm sorry, Sheriff. But Sheik Efraim is correct. He can't talk about the reason he's here."

Wolf raised his black brows. "So am I to assume that your office is involved in this, Callie?"

"I'm sorry, Jake. I really can't confirm or deny anything. I came home to visit my dad and brothers."

"I've never known you to be uncooperative, Callie."

"I'm not being uncooperative. Neither is Sheik Efraim. We told you everything we know."

"I doubt that. A man was killed. Murdered. And why he was here in this country, what he was doing, who might want to stop him from doing it, all of that is important to my investigation. You know that." He leaned forward, peering directly into Callie's eyes, talking to her as if she was the only one in the room.

But even though the sheriff's words were directed at Callie, Efraim got the feeling the man was noting every movement he made, looking for signs of guilt.

He stood straight, arms hanging still at his sides. He smoothed his features into the expressionless mask he wore during tense policy talks in his country, and the weekly games of American poker he had enjoyed with Fahad, and Fahad's brother Kateb.

"I'm not trying to hide anything from you, Jake. Sheik Efraim and the others are here on vacation. Let's just leave it at that."

"He and a handful of other royals enjoy vacationing together? That's the official story?" The sheriff shook his head. "It's gone beyond that, Callie. Way beyond. Things are serious. People are dying. From the sound of tonight's events, your own brother could have been one of them. You have to tell me everything. If I'm to protect the people of Wind River County and uphold the law, I need to know what's going on here."

"You just have to take my word for it, Jake," Callie said in a calm voice.

"And your role in his vacation?" The sheriff held up a hand.

"I told you—"

"That you're just here to visit your family, I know. Come on, Callie. I'm not that gullible."

"Then think of me as a goodwill ambassador."

Efraim choked back a chuckle. She certainly was. Of all the Americans he'd ever met, she was the one bright beacon. The one person who made him feel as if the whole country wasn't aligned against him.

All the more reason he needed to get his head together.

As if on cue, the office door swung open, and Callie's father stepped in. "There are some men at the door, Sheriff. They want to talk to you."

The sheriff frowned. "Thanks, Clay. Can you tell them I'll be there in a moment?"

Callie's father nodded and left the way he'd come.

The sheriff pushed to his feet and leveled his black eyes on Efraim. A couple of inches taller, Sheriff Wolf was an imposing figure. He probably had intimidated more than a few criminals in his term as sheriff.

Too bad Efraim was not easily intimidated. "You might as well go out and talk to your men, Sheriff. I have nothing left to say, and I really have to get back to the resort."

The door flew open. Two men in plain suits and short haircuts stepped into the room. The one half a step ahead stopped in front of Efraim. "I hope that's not the case, Mr. Aziz, because the questions are only beginning."

CALLIE SHOT to her feet. She stepped toward the men. They looked like central casting's idea of an FBI agent, but she asked the question anyway. "Can I see some ID?"

The first to enter the room, a bland-looking man with short gray hair, flipped open his ID and handed it to her. The other didn't move. Apparently his job was to fade into the woodwork and observe.

She looked at the name. "Frank Priebus."

"That's right." He held out his hand for her to return the ID.

Callie gave it to Jake Wolf instead. She doubted the sheriff could do any more than she could to stop the men from talking to Efraim, but at least she had to give him the opportunity to try.

He glanced at the identification and thrust it back at Priebus. "I'm in the middle of a murder investigation here."

"No need to get territorial, Sheriff. You can have him back when we're done with him."

"And when will that be?"

"That depends on Mr. Aziz." Priebus shot Efraim a pointed look, as if he should know what was expected. Tilting his wrist, he checked his watch before turning his attention back to Jake. "When our issues are resolved, you can drive down to Denver and pick him up."

Callie's blood pressure spiked. "I'm sorry, gentlemen. If you think you can waltz out of here with the sheik, you're sadly mistaken."

"We didn't drive all the way out to your ranch for our health, ma'am. We're taking Mr. Aziz to the branch office. He has some serious issues to untangle."

Despite the years she'd worked for the U.S. government, she was still amazed at how much some government agents could talk and still divulge nothing. "What kind of serious issues?"

"We're not at liberty to talk about the specifics."

"I'm with the Office of Foreign Affairs. All I have to do is call the secretary and she'll see that you're reassigned to someplace a lot less interesting than Denver."

Priebus gave her a bored look. "Call away. And in the meantime, you can explain to us what interest a diplomat like you has with a man like this."

A muscle along Efraim's jaw tensed.

If someone had told Callie this day could get worse, she wouldn't have believed it. But somehow things were getting worse with every minute that passed. She longed to help him, comfort him, even simply give him a little space to grieve his cousin's death. But so far she had failed to provide him any of those things. So far, her plan to ride to her family's ranch and call the sheriff had done nothing but cause him more pain. First the fear, hate and suspicion from her dad and brothers, then Jake Wolf's questioning, now the FBI's threats to take him into custody... By the time this night was over, Efraim would not want anything to do with the United States. He wouldn't allow the acronym COIN uttered in his presence.

And he certainly wouldn't want her.

She pushed away the personal pain that thought brought. She had a duty to keep the COIN alliance together. She had an obligation to Efraim as a compassionate human being. Her personal feelings had no place.

And in light of how Efraim must feel about everything American right now—her included—no hope.

"If you won't answer, I'd be happy to call your office."

At least Priebus's threats were getting a lot easier to handle. He must be getting tired. "Call away. My office is as good at playing its cards close to the vest as yours is."

Priebus flashed her a salesman's smile. "Then maybe you'd like to enlighten me?"

She tossed back a phony smile of her own. "I can't discuss it with you."

"Discuss what, Callie?" Jake Wolf eyed her. "You said you were just welcoming the sheik on his vacation. What about a simple vacation is there to discuss?"

She didn't look at the sheriff. Jake Wolf was a good man. She'd even contributed to his campaign, eager to get the former, crooked sheriff ousted and an honest lawman in the office. Before this, she thought his dogged pursuit of the truth and refusal to cut anyone slack was a good thing. He was cleaning up a county steeped in corruption. But tonight his refusal to simply take her at her word was wearing thin. "I am here to welcome the sheik. And I would like to point out how unwelcoming all of you are being."

Priebus let out a hard guffaw. "You would have us welcome Mr. Aziz? I can see the Office of Foreign Affairs is a little behind the times."

If there was anything she hated, it was being condescended to. Especially by a man who didn't know what the hell he was muddling into. "If you'll call my office…"

"Tell you what. We'll call when we get Mr. Aziz to Denver."

"You aren't taking Mr. Aziz to Denver."

"You don't have the authority to stop us."

"I wouldn't bet on that if I were you." If Priebus wasn't going to call the secretary, she would.

Sheriff Wolf stepped up to Priebus. Taller than the FBI agent by several inches, Jake towered over the man. And next to Priebus's staid suit and metrosexual vibe, Jake's boots, well-fitting Wranglers and howling wolf belt buckle made him look rough. Almost dangerous. "What has this man done that involves the FBI?"

"I can't share that information with you."

"Do you even know? Or is that the reason you're so set on scampering back to your superiors in Denver?"

Priebus's smart aleck attitude was gone, replaced by an emotionless void of a man strictly following procedure instead of thought. "We need to talk to him."

"Then you can do that here."

Priebus glanced around the room. "We require someplace a little more secure."

Callie had an idea. It wouldn't solve the problem, but it might give her a chance to make some calls. She just hoped Jake would go along with it. "How about the sheriff's department? Or isn't a jail secure enough for you?"

Efraim shifted his eyes to look at her.

She tried to give him a look conveying that it would be okay, but she wasn't sure she succeeded.

Jake paused for a moment, then nodded. "You can use our interrogation room. And when you're done asking whatever it is you so badly need to ask, you won't have to drive him all the way back to Dumont."

Priebus gave him a weak version of the insincere smile he'd flashed Callie earlier. "That's generous of you."

Jake shrugged. "I always try to cooperate with federal law enforcement."

"Do you now? That would be a change from the last sheriff around here."

Of course. Now Callie could see why the FBI had come to Wind River County spoiling for a fight. They hadn't fully realized how much the guard had changed. "Sheriff Wolf is a fair man. I trust you are, too, Special Agent."

"Oh, I'm very fair. When fairness is warranted."

Although still talking to Priebus, she glanced at Efraim. "I trust in this case, you'll find it is."

Priebus walked around Jake and stepped to Efraim's side. "Shall we, Mr. Aziz?" He gave an exaggerated bow.

Callie shook her head. She supposed this was Priebus's way to save face, but it certainly wouldn't improve Efraim's frame of mind. She needed to get to a phone and get this FBI nightmare over with before things got worse, although at this point, worse seemed unlikely. "You'll drive Mr. Aziz, Sheriff?"

"Of course I will." Jake nodded to Efraim.

He'd been standing stock-still, watching the fireworks. Now he angled his body toward Jake in a small bow.

As they walked from the office and out the front door, Callie tried to catch Efraim's eye. She wanted to let him know things would be okay. That she'd move heaven and earth to make these problems go away, at least the problems she had some power over. But he didn't glance back. He didn't say a word. He just marched from the house as he'd marched in front of her father's gun.

As she stood in the doorway and watched him climb into Jake's white SUV, she wondered if this was the end. For COIN. For the economic recovery of Nadar. For the feelings that had swept over her when she and Efraim kissed.

Her father stepped in front of her, and closed the front door. He turned his eyes on her, blue like her own. "Callie, we need to talk."

"Listen, Dad, I have to make a call to my office."

"You have to talk to me. Now."

She knew that tone, and she'd learned a long time ago that it was best to face it early than let his anger fester. Too bad this time she couldn't do what was best. "I'm sorry, Dad. I have to make a call. It's vital." She grasped the satellite phone from his desk and started up the stairs to her room.

"*He's* vital to you," her dad grumbled behind her. "That's exactly what we need to talk about."

And here she thought things couldn't get worse.

Chapter Six

It took over an hour, mostly spent waiting on hold, showering and putting on clean clothing, and calling back, before Callie was confident her message made it to the Secretary of Foreign Affairs. The thought of Efraim sitting at the sheriff's interrogation room fielding questions he couldn't answer from that dunderheaded FBI agent, Priebus, was too upsetting to bear. If he'd had a bad opinion of Americans before this, she could just guess how bright his attitude was now. She'd be lucky if he didn't back out of COIN all together and return to Nadar.

Barking clamored outside the house, not deep and threatening, but light yips of excited welcome.

Her brothers were back.

She plunked the phone on the bedside table of her childhood room. She had no desire to talk to Brent right now. But the return of Brent and Joe reminded her of the other thing she had to do...besides face her father.

She had to make sure Timmy was okay.

She left her room and walked down the hall. Timmy's door was closed. No sound came from the room. She rapped on the door with her knuckles, hoping he could hear her despite the fact that he was probably listening to music and wouldn't be able to hear anything short of a nuclear explosion.

A moment passed. She hated to just burst in, even though she knew her brothers did it all the time. It was different with a sister, though. Especially one so much older.

When Timmy was growing up, she was more like his second mom than a sibling. And now that she'd left home, whenever she came back for a visit, Timmy fell all over himself trying to impress her. As if he really had to try.

She knocked again, this time louder. "Tim?"

The door opened and her little brother peered out of a dark room. If she hadn't just seen him this morning, she didn't know if she would recognize him. An angry scrape marred his chin. One eye was puffy and starting to purple. His skin was red under his tan.

Her dad had said he'd flipped the ATV, but with all that had happened, she hadn't had a chance to process what that meant. "Oh, Timmy, you're hurt." She gathered his lanky, teenage body in her arms and held him as tightly as she dared.

"Callie, I was so worried about you."

She felt something wet on her neck and realized he was crying. She held him a minute longer, then pulled back to look at him.

He turned away from her and retreated back into the dark room, dashing away his tears with the back of his hand.

She waited until he'd covered the evidence of his crying, then rested her hand on the wall switch. She wanted to see him, make sure he really was okay. "Can I turn on the light?"

"Sure."

She flipped the switch. Timmy looked even more battered in the overhead light. "Maybe you should see a doctor."

"I'm okay. I'm just glad you are, too."

She gave him a smile, although she wasn't sure she really was okay. She felt shaky deep in her chest, and she couldn't honestly say whether the feeling was caused by the precarious status of the COIN summit or the memory of Efraim's kiss.

At least she had Timmy to focus on at the moment. "You need to get some aloe on that sunburn."

"Yes, Mom." He gave her a lopsided smile.

"Brent and Joe are back."

His smile faded. "I doubt Dad will let me go out on the ATV again."

"At least not alone." She still wasn't sure what Timmy was thinking, venturing out by himself. Not that she could talk. She'd found Efraim in the badlands, but she'd left the ranch alone. "We'd better both be a little more careful, okay? There's some nasty stuff happening out there. A man was murdered tonight."

"Murdered?" Timmy looked stricken.

She hated that he was so young and yet had to face this stuff. Teenagers had enough problems to deal with. "The sheriff is handling it. He'll find who did it."

"The sheriff?" Timmy sat on the edge of his bed, as if his legs were too weak to hold him up anymore.

"Sheriff Wolf was here tonight along with the crime

scene investigator and the coroner. Didn't you hear them?"

"I was listening to music." He held up his iPod. "And I fell asleep."

Probably just as well. After all Timmy had been through, he likely needed the rest. And with the FBI's sudden entrance, Jake hadn't gotten around to asking Timmy about the attack on him. "Well, don't worry about it. Really. Jake will take care of it. And he'll be back."

"Why?"

"To look at your ATV and talk to you about what happened. There's a chance that whoever murdered that man is the one who shot out your tire."

He stared at her and said nothing.

She sat next to him on the bed. Maybe she shouldn't have told him about the possible connection to the murderer. The fact that both of them had come so close to a murderer had freaked her out. It might be too much for a seventeen-year-old to handle. "You don't have to worry about it, Timmy. Okay? This killer, he's not after you. But you might want to stick around the ranch for a while? Ease my mind a little?"

"Okay."

She held out her arms.

He gave her a hug. "But only if you promise me you'll be careful, too."

"You bet, Tim. You bet."

When she left Timmy, she felt pretty sure he'd go along with all she'd asked in the days and weeks to come. Her dad wasn't so cooperative. As soon as Joe left for home and Brent and Russ came in from putting up the horses, he pinned down Callie with a frown and an, "It's time to talk. Now."

She met her father's stern eyes. There was no getting out of the confrontation this time. She followed him back into his study, leaving Russ telling Brent and Tim about the dead Arab and the visit from the FBI.

Callie's dad closed the door behind them. "Sit down, Cal."

"I'm okay."

He let out a heavy sigh. "Let's not start arguing about sitting or standing. I have a feeling we'll find plenty more important things to argue about here shortly."

She perched on the edge of a leather recliner.

Her father took the other. "I know this sheik has something to do with your job, that all of those royal types up at the Wind River Resort do, too." He held up a hand before she could open her mouth. "Don't bother denying it or handing me all that bullcrap you were shoveling for the sheriff and FBI. Just hear me out."

She pressed her lips together and sat back a little in her chair. Giving him his say was probably the least she could do after bringing murder and the law down on his ranch tonight. She could afford to listen.

"I don't know if you recognize it yet or if you're still fooling yourself, but I can see in your eyes that whatever is with you and this sheik, it goes deeper than your job."

She jerked back to the edge of the chair. "What?"

"You and the sheik. You care about him."

She could feel the blood inch up her neck and heat flush into her cheeks. She pushed memories of their kiss deep to the back of her mind. "I hardly know him."

"I'm glad you recognize that fact. I hope you really believe that and aren't just spouting it for my sake."

Did she really believe it? It was true. They'd just met. But she had to admit, she felt she understood him better than people she'd known for years. And she felt like he understood her, as well. "He's the leader of an island nation in the Mediterranean. It's my job to welcome him to the United States."

"I told you not to hand me that, Callie. I've seen how you look at him when he talks. I've seen how you focus on him no matter who else is in the room. I may just be a simple rancher, but I know what I see. And I know where that kind of thing is going. Someplace that will only cause heartache and tragedy."

"Heartache and… Dad, you're reading way too much into this. I pay attention to him because I need to know what he's thinking. I am worried he has a skewed opinion of America and Americans. Being interrogated by the FBI is not going to help."

"For such a smart girl, you don't get it, do you, Callie?"

"Don't get what?"

"They attacked us. They are trying to kill us, to ruin our way of life."

Callie clawed her hand back through her hair. She'd had this discussion with so many short-sighted, frightened people since 9/11. She didn't want to have it with her dad…again. "Who is *they,* Dad?"

"You know exactly who *they* is. And this guy you can't take your eyes off, he's one of 'em."

"Arabs."

He tilted his head, conceding.

"That's racist."

"I'm not saying all of them. But him? You said yourself that he leads a country and has a skewed opinion of America. I'll bet that country is pretty anti-American."

She couldn't argue that point. There was a powerful anti-American sentiment in Nadar. And she didn't want to try to explain to her father why that was so, starting with the way American corporations led by the U.S. government had taken advantage of Efraim's father. It would be an impossible task. And in the end, he would just see it as proving his point.

"I also saw how he reacted to us. To the sheriff. To those FBI stiffs. He has a big chip on his shoulder, that one."

"He hardly said a word."

"You don't have to hear a man talk to read his attitude."

"If he felt defensive, it might be because you guys gave him plenty of reason."

"Be that as it may, there's no love lost between him and our people, Callie. You've got to see that."

If she had to listen to any more of this hatred and prejudice and fear, she was going to scream. "He's not our enemy. His people aren't our enemy."

"You say that, but he doesn't see it that way. And neither do your brothers and I."

Tears surged into her eyes. She blinked them back. Her dad was right. He and her brothers and Efraim, they were quite a bunch. All of them seemed set on hating the other. And where did that leave her?

She'd always had this problem, ever since she was

a little girl. Half of her was a ranch girl, a red-blooded American who lived for rodeo and wide-open spaces and fireworks on the Fourth of July. The other half loved the people and traditions she'd found all over the world. The fascination of talking to people different from her was exhilarating. It opened the world like nothing she'd ever known. She longed for peace and knowledge and the challenge of seeing life from a different point of view.

She'd never found anyone who could embrace both sides of her. Accept the cowgirl and the world-traveling diplomat. Recognize that being a real American was bigger than clinging to one narrow view, and that being a citizen of the world also meant being able to appreciate a simple country life.

"Jim Borcher called after you today."

Oh, God, not now.

"He really likes you, you know. And he's a good man."

"Dad, no."

"Then how about Jake Wolf? He's a good guy, tall, women seem to think he's pretty good-looking. And a sheriff now. You could do worse."

She had to get out of here. Not only did she need to drive to the sheriff's department, but also this conversation was crossing the line of embarrassing and heading into the realm of painful. She wished her dad would concentrate on his own love life and leave hers alone. "Let's talk about Helen. From what Joe says, you two are seeing a lot of each other. She seems to make you really happy."

"You know Helen. She's great. But don't change the subject."

"Dad, I don't need a matchmaker. Please."

"You need something, Callie. And it's not a sheik who hates everything you are and everyone you care about."

EFRAIM SAT in a hard chair bolted to the floor and stared at the camera peering at him from the corner of the room. On American television shows, the suspect always got to sit with a table between him and the interrogator. Apparently they didn't believe in that setup in Wind River County, Wyoming.

He felt exposed, vulnerable, sitting in this chair in front of the camera. He knew that was the idea. Prevent him from hiding anything, even the nervous bounce of his leg. Make him feel like his thoughts were laid bare. He didn't like it. Not a bit.

He couldn't wait to get the hell out of this country and back to Nadar. A place were he wasn't looked at as a criminal merely for the color of his skin and the origins of his blood. A country where he was in control of his own future.

And the future of everyone else.

He tried to ignore the pang at the thought of his country's bleak economic future without a COIN agreement, but the effort was futile.

Unless…

As soon as he got the chance, he'd call Darek. Prince of Saruk, a larger island nation in the same region, Darek had honored his father's wishes and refused to be part of the COIN compact. Darek was surprised when

Efraim went along with the agreement despite Nadar's history with the United States. Surprised and unhappy. But despite his disagreement with Efraim and the other leaders of COIN, he'd called to express his worry about Amir. He'd reached out when it had meant the most, and Efraim was grateful for that.

Yes, he would call Darek. Darek would have ideas of how to shape the future of Nadar without COIN. And just maybe some of those ideas would bear fruit, and Efraim could leave America behind for good.

The door creaked open and the FBI agent from the ranch stepped inside. A woman followed. Short brown hair, dark suit and expressionless eyes, she looked like a younger and feminine version of Special Agent Priebus.

Maybe FBI agents weren't born but manufactured.

The woman took a chair a few feet from Efraim. Priebus remained standing. "Mr. Aziz. Let's stop with the nonsense now, shall we?"

Efraim crooked a brow at the man. "Are you referring to your nonsense? Because I haven't spewed any recently."

Priebus shook his head and glanced down at a thick manila folder in his hands. "How did you manage to get into the United States?"

"I flew." If they wanted nonsense, he could throw in the old joke about his arms being tired, but his mood was well past joking.

"That's interesting." Again he glanced at the folder, as if he couldn't remember what he was going to say from one moment to the next. "There is no record of you on any flights coming into the country."

"It was a chartered flight."

"Chartered? By whom?"

Efraim let out a heavy breath. He wasn't sure how much he should tell the FBI. The COIN summit was top secret. Or at least it was supposed to be before the explosion that might have claimed Amir's life. An explosion they'd later learned was meant to kill all five members of COIN. If Callie was here, she could manage these agents, tell them only what they were cleared to know. Without her, he had no way to judge.

Without her…

He pushed Callie to the back of his mind, as well. Kissing her had been a mistake. It was a romantic fantasy, he and Callie. He was too old for fantasies.

"Are you refusing to answer, sir?"

"The United States government. They arranged for my flight."

"This is a serious question, Mr. Aziz."

"And that was a serious answer. Really, you people need to talk to one another."

"You are on a terrorist watch list. Why would the U.S. government arrange for you to come here?"

"Terrorist watch list?" That was a new one for him. "I'm not on your list."

"You are. It's right here." Priebus paged through the folder in his hands. Finally reaching the end of his sheaf of paper, he looked up at the younger female version of himself. "Joy?"

The woman who looked like she could have been given just about any name other than Joy opened her folder and began flipping paper.

Efraim looked down at his hands folded in his lap.

Sheriff Wolf had insisted on taking him to the hospital to see a doctor. And while his ribs were taped and he was given some painkillers, his hands were still stained with Fahad's blood. The dull, rust color lined every crease and swirl of fingerprint.

"Found it."

Efraim glanced up in time to see the woman hand a thick stack to Priebus. Paper flipping resumed.

Maybe they'd never heard of computers, Efraim thought drily. Although he'd bet if the aim was to rattle the suspect, a stack of paper was more intimidating.

Finally the man seemed to find what he was after. He looked up at Efraim. "Here. Faraj Aziz. Lived in Afghanistan for a year. And here's a nice list of known contacts, including some pretty high ranking names in terrorist circles."

"Yes." Those were the facts, facts of which he couldn't pretend to be proud.

"So you're admitting all these things are true?"

"They are true. But I am not Faraj Aziz. I am Efraim Aziz, acting leader of Nadar. Faraj is my brother."

"Your brother?" Priebus looked at him as if he didn't believe a word.

"Even Arabs have brothers."

The FBI agent scoffed. "The question is, does Faraj Aziz have a brother, and is he any less radical?"

"My brother is a little…wild, angry. It is true. But since I am not him, and I'm not very close to him, I don't see what else I can tell you. Perhaps you have a file somewhere on me. Perhaps you could look that up and then tell me if you think I'm a danger to you and your country."

Priebus gestured to the door with a sway of his head, and Joy stood and left. Priebus paused, hand on the door, and glanced back at Efraim. "We'll be back."

Efraim gave him a phony smile, thinking of the old movie quote delivered by Arnold Schwarzenegger. "No problem. I'll wait."

The door closed behind them and left him alone with the camera once again. More time to contemplate pulling out of COIN and leaving the United States as soon as Fahad's murderer was found…as soon as Amir was found…as soon as Efraim made the bastards attacking his friends and his family pay.

If not for the rift between them when Darek first learned of COIN, Efraim and his friend might have reached an understanding before this whole mess began. Before he'd been cajoled into trusting the Americans. Before he'd started down this path. He needed to talk to Darek as soon as possible. There might be an option for Nadar yet. An option that didn't include trusting people who hated everything he was.

A knock sounded on the door once again, but this time it didn't immediately swing open.

"Found the files on me already, did you?" Efraim called. "Well, come in. I can't wait to have a peek."

The door pushed open, but it wasn't the FBI who stepped into the room.

She'd showered, changed into a clean blue T-shirt and pulled her hair back, making her eyes look bigger and deeper than the sea surrounding Nadar. "I already know what's in your files. Believe me, they aren't as interesting as the man himself."

"Callie." Efraim pulled in the sight of her along with a jittery breath.

She scooped the air toward the open door. "Come on, let's get out of here before they pull strings that outrank the strings I pulled."

Chapter Seven

Efraim hadn't realized how comfortable it would be letting Callie take the wheel until he was sitting in the passenger seat of her pickup. Too bad his comfort level didn't extend further than that.

Not that he wasn't grateful to Callie for getting him out of the ridiculous situation with the FBI. He was. But he needed time to think before she cornered him about his commitment to COIN, time to think and a second perspective. And somehow he doubted they would manage the long drive from Dumont to the resort in silence.

She scooped up a hatbox and a pair of old cowboy boots lying at his feet and transferred them to the backseat of the king cab. "Sorry about the truck. I know it's not the kind of vehicle a sheik is used to riding in." She gestured to a windshield pocked with dead bugs and clouded with dust.

"It's fine."

"It belongs to my brother Russ. He uses it to haul to rodeos."

He suppressed the urge to ask which brother—the one who hated him or the one who hated him more.

She strapped on her seat belt and started the pickup. Soft country music drifted from the radio. A welcome break in the silence. Efraim only wished the soaring steel guitar could dispel the tension hanging in the air.

Callie shifted into gear and pulled out onto the street. "The truck isn't all I'm sorry about. I'm so sorry for your loss, Efraim."

He stared out the windshield, watching the town roll away and the open country stretch ahead. "Thank you. I'll convey your sympathies to Fahad's brother, as well."

"Thank you. And there's more."

He wished he could say something, head her off before she started discussing things he hadn't yet come to terms with, asking questions he wasn't quite ready to tackle. He didn't know if his English was deficient or the day had been too harrowing and exhausting. Whatever the reason, he simply couldn't find the words.

"I'm sorry for what the FBI put you through and for the sheriff's questions, but most of all, I'm sorry for my family. I was hoping they would show you more American hospitality."

He brushed away her apology with a wave of his hand, although it felt good to hear her say it. "It does not matter."

"I'm afraid it might."

"How is that?"

"The COIN compact is very important for the future of Nadar."

Just what he was hoping to avoid. He held up a hand, not wanting her to continue on that path. He didn't want to talk about this with Callie. Not until he knew where he wanted to go. Not until he'd laid out his options, at least in his own mind. "About the COIN compact. I have some thinking to do."

"I was afraid you were leaning in that direction."

"What direction? Thinking?"

"I recognize your tone. You're considering pulling out of COIN."

He couldn't deny it. He only wished he could talk to Darek before getting embroiled in this conversation. "I'm not prepared to talk about my intentions at this time."

"You don't have to be so formal. I promise this is not an official meeting."

He gave her a glance. "Trying to lower my defenses?"

"If that's what it takes to get you to hear what I have to say, then yes."

He could think of many things she could do to lower his defenses. Not that he'd be listening to her arguments about COIN if she chose any of the actions on his list.

He pushed those particular thoughts out of his mind. "Okay, I'm listening."

Keeping her gaze glued to the ribbon of road ahead, she set her chin. "I know these past few days have been hard on you, and that today was the worst. I can't blame you for feeling negatively toward my country after what has happened here and the way people and the authorities have treated you. But these past few days are not indicative of what my country is and how an agreement like COIN can help stabilize Nadar's economy and political situation."

"What do you want, Callie? You want me to promise Nadar will be part of COIN?"

Wind whistled through Callie's lowered window. Highway hummed under the tires. Outside the pickup, vegetation changed from the low sage of the plains to Russian olive, aspen and even a few pine and fir. Finally Callie answered. "I want you to trust me."

"It's your country and countrymen I don't trust."

"I was afraid you'd say that."

"And you have a prepared response?"

She shook her head. "Not one that will work."

"You know I had serious reservations about the COIN agreement from the beginning."

Callie let out a sigh. "I'd hoped your trip to Wyoming would make some of those reservations go away. I'd hoped it would improve your opinion of America."

Now he didn't know what to say. Callie was proud of her country and she loved it passionately. He could understand that. He even admired it. But no matter what he thought about her love for the United States, he couldn't say that he shared it.

Finally she broke the silence. "But it hasn't, has it? Improved your opinion?"

"It's been a hard day." As hard as any he'd lived through.

She pulled her gaze from the road and focused for a second on him. "Do you think you can trust me?"

He felt her question as a pang behind his breastbone. "I want to."

"Then know I won't let my country do to you what it did to your father."

"It's not that simple. As good as you are at your job, you don't singlehandedly control your government."

"No, but I can promise if I see anything wrong or hear of anything that might be detrimental to your people, I will tell you. No matter what it means for my job."

He wanted to believe she'd choose him over her job, over her country, over her family, over everything. He wanted a lot of things where Callie was concerned. Things that were impossible to ask, impossible to believe. Things that were out of the control of either of them.

He peered out the side window and stared at the blur of a split rail fence whipping past. Nadar was a small island and filled with people. Any drive along the cliffs or walks on the beaches and one saw houses and villages and people wherever one looked. In Wyoming it seemed they could drive for miles or ride for hours and see no one at all.

"You're not convinced."

He didn't answer. He didn't know what to say that she wouldn't feel she had to refute.

"Then I'll make a deal with you. Just between us, you and me."

He looked back to her. "A deal?"

Her eyes shifted to him and then back to the road. She swallowed, the gentle movement of her throat visible in the dashboard lights. "I doubt you're planning to just up and leave Wyoming. Not until Amir is found and not until you see Fahad's murderer brought to justice."

He wasn't sure her version of justice was identical to his, but he nodded just the same.

"Then there's no reason for you to make a decision

on the future of COIN until then. Until it's time to go back to Nadar."

"I suppose not."

"Then here's my proposal. If you stick with me on COIN, I'll do everything I can to help you find out who killed Fahad."

"I can't make a deal like that."

She pulled one hand from the wheel and held it up to stop him. "I'm not asking you to agree to any kind of terms. Just listen to the proposals, participate in the ne-gotiations with the other leaders. In the end, if you don't believe COIN will benefit your people, you're welcome to walk away. I just want you to stay for the summit and give the compact a fair hearing."

"If the summit ever takes place."

She set her chin. "It will."

If it was up to her, he was sure that would be true. Problem was, only so much was up to her. "You just want me to stay?"

She pulled her focus from the road, just for a second, the briefest glance, but a shiver blew over his skin, cold and then hot. "Yes, Efraim. More than I can say."

THE MAIN LODGE of the Wind River Ranch and Resort soared out of the landscape, a palace of stone and rough-hewn logs that sought to match the grandeur of the mountains themselves. While Callie maintained that it didn't quite measure up in *that* ambition, she couldn't help feeling a little in awe over the beauty and opulence of the place.

This was a guest ranch fit for royalty, yet it held a rugged charm that was pure American West. But as much as she loved this place, as she accompanied Efraim into the soaring great room, she couldn't fully appreciate its beauty.

Even though Efraim had agreed to the deal she'd offered, she couldn't shake the feeling that he was mired in doubt. Doubt about COIN, doubt that the authorities would find Amir, doubt that the American justice system would deliver for Fahad, and most hurtful of all, doubt in her. And try as she might, she couldn't think of a way to prove to him that he could trust her.

On the entire drive back, she'd hemmed and hawed about what Fahad had said to her before he died. Just thinking about it made her unspeakably sad. She hadn't told Efraim. She didn't know what she would say.

Your cousin hated me? He thought I was trying to manipulate you? He thought you shouldn't trust me?

In the end, she hadn't said anything. Until she could figure out some way to prove herself to Efraim, it seemed as if admitting Fahad's dying words would be akin to telling Efraim to never trust her again.

"Efraim. Ms. McGuire. In here." Stefan Lutece motioned them into a small conference room. A gleaming wood table stretched the length of the room, flanked by comfortable leather chairs. The setting for the COIN summit, if it ever took place.

They joined Stefan, and Sebastian and Antoine Cavanaugh in the room. Antoine closed the door behind them. When she'd called from the Seven M, Callie had explained everything that had happened to Stefan. Judging from Sebastian's and Antoine's grim expressions, he'd passed information on to them as she'd requested.

"The sheriff's just arrived."

Callie nodded. Jake had left as soon as she'd arrived to rescue Efraim from the FBI. She'd guessed the sheriff had been heading to the Wind River Ranch. "He'll want to look through Fahad's belongings."

"Yes, Jane is with him," Stefan said, referring to Jane Cameron, a crime scene investigator. Jane and Stefan had been through a hell of their own recently. Callie was glad to see them still spending every spare moment together, obviously deeply in love.

Stefan continued. "I think we have to assume this was an attack on you, Efraim. That whoever shot Fahad was aiming to take out your security."

Sebastian pulled out a chair as if to sit, but remained standing. "The car bomb might have only hurt Amir, but it was meant for all of us. That's what the text said."

Callie glanced at the nods coming from around the room. She knew about the text message Jane had found on another investigator's phone. Bomb failed. Intended for all the coalition. Move to plan B. She glanced at Prince Stefan. "Has Jane or the authorities discovered who sent the text?"

Stefan shook his head. "Not yet."

"I can guess what plan B is," Sebastian continued. "After Amir disappeared, there were attempts to kill Stefan. Now Efraim. If they can't get us all with one bomb, they are going to try to take us out one at a time. The question is, who is *they?*"

"Not a simple question," Sebastian's twin brother Antoine said. He looked at Stefan. "It could be Russian organized crime."

Stefan nodded. He'd had a close call with a sniper, a

man wearing a tattoo known as the type of art preferred by the Russian mob.

Callie added her nod to his. "The Russian mob is known to be active in the area surrounding your island nations. There have even been rumors that they have had dealings with the king of Saruk in the past, although those can't be substantiated. Yet to date, they hadn't been able to gain a strong foothold in any of COIN or in Saruk. Not that they aren't still trying. Maybe this is their latest attempt."

Efraim shook his head. "There's one problem with that theory."

"What is that?" Antoine asked.

"The man who shot Fahad wasn't Russian."

Callie frowned. He hadn't mentioned that. Of course, they hadn't had much of a chance to talk since her family "helped" Efraim at gunpoint, the sheriff grilled him and the FBI took him away. "How do you know?"

"He spoke to me."

"He spoke?" Callie repeated. Efraim hadn't told her that, and she had to wonder why.

"He spoke with an American accent. His accent was familiar." He glanced at Callie out of the corner of his eye. "He sounded like he might be from the area."

His words clanged through Callie's head like a hard blow. A local? How could that be possible? "No."

Efraim bowed his head. "I'm sorry."

So he thought the shooter was one of her neighbors? One of her friends? *Her family?* She shook her head. She couldn't accept that. There must be another explanation. "So an American could be working for the Russian mob. Or it could be a mobster who's an American citizen."

Efraim nodded. The lines bracketing his eyes softened a little, as if he was as relieved to have found a possible explanation as she was.

"There was a group protesting our presence in front of the courthouse," Stefan said in a low voice. "Americans who believe we are here to learn how to enrich uranium for bombs."

Callie waved her hands, trying to erase any horrible images Stefan's words might conjure. "I saw them. They're just a bunch of people whose fear has been stoked by cable TV. They're not violent. Just afraid."

Antoine shook his head and leaned back in his chair. Although he and Sebastian were twins, they had always struck Callie as very different men. Sebastian seemed like a bold and strong leader, always quick to protect anyone in need. Antoine was much darker, and she suspected his years in Barajas's intelligence, particularly his expertise in interrogation, was what gave him that unsettling edge.

She met his eyes. "You don't agree?"

"In my experience, some of the most violent people are those who are afraid. Like dogs that bite."

She didn't want to hear this. She didn't want to think about any of it. But she knew she had to. "I will look into the protesters."

Efraim and Sebastian opened their mouths at the same time as if readying their own protests.

She held up a hand to stop them. "You don't need to protect me. Either of you. Think about it. You're the people they're afraid of. I'm a local girl. I can handle it better than any of the four of you can. You best focus on finding out more about the Russian mob."

"We can call Darek," Efraim said. "See what problems he's had with the Russians."

Callie's stomach tensed. The last she'd heard, there was tension between Darek and the royals whose countries were part of COIN. Apparently that had changed. "Darek?" She looked up at Efraim.

He glanced away and began studying one of the Western paintings stretching across the boardroom's richly paneled walls.

"He called when he heard about Amir's disappearance," Stefan explained. "He has reopened the lines of communication."

Callie nodded, trying to hide her worry. If she were more naive, she might want to believe this new communication could lead to Saruk joining the compact along with the other four smaller island nations. But although she had no reason to mistrust Darek, who she knew was close with Efraim, Darek's father was another matter. In all his dealings, the king of Saruk was less than predictable.

She just hoped the leaders in this room could talk Darek into joining them and not the other way around. She was especially worried about Efraim.

She glanced up at him. He was still gazing at the painting as if it was the most fascinating thing he'd ever seen. "Efraim, can I have a word with you?"

He looked back down at her, his expression that of a man who knew he'd have to face something unpleasant. "Certainly."

Callie's stomach sank as they left the others. She'd hoped she could convince Efraim to trust her. She didn't want him to see her as demanding or controlling. As soon as they were alone in the corridor leading to his suite, she broke the tense silence. "I think it's wonderful you are talking to Darek again."

"He doesn't agree that the United States should have a role in negotiations."

"I know. Maybe you four and Amir can convince him this time." She gave him a smile.

Efraim didn't smile back.

She had to figure out a way to reach him. Obviously talking about Darek, even if she played up the positive, was not going to cut it. "You should have told me that the man who jumped you was American."

"You really wanted to know?"

"No. The whole idea makes me feel shaky. But I'll face it."

Efraim pressed his lips together.

It wasn't a smile exactly, but an expression of satisfaction. But it was enough to make Callie feel warmth surge through her. "I told you I'll stick by you, and I mean it."

Efraim reached toward her. His fingers brushed her hand, as if he'd wanted to hold it but held back. He looked straight ahead down the hall.

Callie tore her gaze away. A man was rushing toward them. She recognized him as part of Efraim's security detail, but this time she recognized more. He was a lot leaner than his brother, his build slight as a teenager, but he had the same facial features, the same dark hair and beard. She felt as if she was staring at a dead man.

It must be Fahad's brother.

"Efraim. Is it true?" Kateb Bahir didn't even glance in

her direction. Eyes riveted to Efraim, he gave the sheik a little bow before he continued. "Is Fahad dead?"

Efraim leveled a somber look on the man. "He is. I am very sorry."

Fahad's brother didn't blink. "The American sheriff wants to look in Fahad's room. I forbid him."

Efraim glanced at Callie. "He doesn't have to listen to us, correct?"

"He'll need to get a warrant if you don't give him permission. A judge will decide if the sheriff has a good enough reason to allow the search. If the judge grants the warrant, Sheriff Wolf can search whether you want him to or not."

Kateb scowled.

Clearly he didn't understand how American justice worked. "The sheriff is looking for evidence that might lead to the person who shot your brother. He might find something that will lead to the killer."

Kateb kept his attention on Efraim. He seemed to hear her, but preferred to act as if she didn't exist.

She was sure hearing that his brother had been killed was hard for Kateb. In light of that, she couldn't take his snub to heart. Besides, in Nadar's past, women weren't allowed to speak directly to men. And she knew that there were some who kept that tradition alive. Maybe Kateb was one.

She pushed the echoes of Fahad's last words from her mind. Kateb could have many reasons for his behavior. It didn't automatically mean he hated her as much as his brother had.

Callie glanced up at him. "It's standard procedure."

Again, his lips pressed into a noncommittal line. His

dark eyes searched hers, and a shiver fanned over her skin. "This warrant," he said. "How long will it take for Wolf to get one?"

Callie glanced at her watch. It was plenty late. Nearly midnight already. "It depends. At this hour, he'll have to wake a judge."

Efraim turned back to Kateb. "Go back to your room, cousin. I will handle things from here."

"I don't trust the Americans. Fahad was head of security for all of the coalition. He might have sensitive information in his room."

"The warrant will outline exactly what the sheriff is looking for," Callie explained. "He is not going to compromise security or any state business."

Kaleb kept his focus on Efraim. "And you trust her? An American?" Kateb asked.

His words hit Callie like a slap. She pretended not to notice.

"I said I will handle things, Kateb."

Kateb narrowed his eyes but didn't move.

"I said go."

Giving another scowl, Fahad's brother stalked away. He pulled out his key card, let himself into his room and slammed the door behind him.

Callie frowned. There was no telling how grief affected a person. Every individual reacted differently to losing a loved one. Her dad had cried openly when her mom died. He'd then become a hermit for years, focusing on the ranch and his children and ignoring the rest of the world. He'd finally moved out of that state in the past year or so, once he'd started dating Helen. Brent had bottled up his grief and run away to the military.

Callie wondered if he'd even cried about their mom yet. She and Joe had reacted more like her father, but instead of shutting themselves away, they'd both thrown themselves into school and career, she becoming a diplomat, he a schoolteacher. Russ and Timmy had been very young and had mostly just taken their cues from everyone else.

Apparently Kateb dealt with grief by becoming angry and distrustful. Or maybe he was always like that. Because she didn't know him, it was hard to tell. But she wouldn't take it personally.

It was Efraim's reaction she was far more interested in. She looked up at him. His dark eyes were focused on Kateb, as if scrolling through his own assessment of his man's behavior. "Efraim?"

His dark gaze flicked to her.

"You know you can trust me, don't you?" She hated sounding so needy, but she couldn't hide it. Fahad's curse had bothered her.... Still bothered her. The thought that he hated her so much, that his brother might hate her, too, made her feel sick. And if Efraim...

She needed Efraim's trust if she was to do her job and facilitate a COIN compact. But as much as she told herself that that was the reason behind her need, she knew that was only a small part.

The truth was, her father had been right. Efraim was important to her and not only because of his tentative commitment to COIN.

Whenever he looked at her, she felt alive. Hyperaware. Drop-dead sexy. Whenever he was near, she thought of their kiss and longed to feel his lips again.

She wanted him to trust her, not only for America's and Nadar's sake, but for her own.

"Come with me." Efraim took her hand this time, his long fingers closing around hers. He led her down another hall, away from Kateb's hard eyes.

At the end of the passage, Jake Wolf and Jane Cameron gathered in a seating area. A woman with curly blond hair stood with them. The head of housekeeping, Callie remembered. Beth Taylor. Obviously Jake had her lined up to let them into Fahad's room once the warrant came through.

Efraim swiped his key card and pulled her into his suite. The sitting room was as beautiful as the rest of the lodge. Wood shelves stretched to the ceiling, loaded with books. Rich leather chairs gathered around a fireplace just waiting for a crackling fire. And through the open door, an opulent king-size bed filled the corner of a luxurious bedroom.

Efraim peered down at her, his dark eyes intense, and for a moment, Callie thought he might kiss her again. She hoped. Her knees felt squishy.

"You said you'll help me find Fahad's murderer. Were you serious?"

"Of course I was. What are you going to do?"

He glanced at a closed door, a door leading to the adjoining room. "Something the sheriff isn't going to like."

A tremor gripped Callie's chest. It made perfect sense Fahad would have the room next to Efraim's. He was charged with protecting the sheik. But even though she knew exactly what Efraim's glance meant, she asked the question anyway. "Does that lead to Fahad's room?"

"I'd like to get a look at his things before the sheriff shuts us out of this investigation."

"Jake won't shut—"

"You know that's not true."

She did. Jake would shut Efraim out. He might consider Efraim a suspect, for all she knew. Of course, if he found out she and Efraim had searched Fahad's room, he'd have good reason for suspecting them.

Efraim took her hand and peered into her eyes. "I know what I'm asking of you, and I'm sorry. But I am in debt to Fahad. I have to do everything I can to find his killer."

"I know." She pushed the words through a tight throat.

"Are you with me on this?"

The tremor grew and spread through her body, down her limbs, until she felt like a shaking mess. She shouldn't go along with this. It wasn't right. It might not even be legal. But with Efraim's eyes on her, she wanted more than anything for him to trust her. To accept her.

There was only one answer she could give. "Yes."

Chapter Eight

Efraim knew his request wasn't fair to Callie. On some level, he also recognized he was testing her. But it wasn't until she said that simple word that he realized how much he needed to hear it from her lips.

He looked down at her, feeling her hand in his, stroking her fingers with his own. Now that she'd committed, they needed to hurry. They needed to get into Fahad's room and get out before the sheriff had a clue what was going on or could stop it. But even knowing time was of the essence, Efraim couldn't move from Callie. He couldn't release her hand. He had to taste her again.

He leaned down and brought his lips to hers.

Her mouth tasted like lemon drops, and she kissed him back, warm and sweet. Blood rushed through his body, making him feel strong, alive, invincible.

It was stupid to kiss her, he knew. Stupid to let himself feel this way. And it muddied everything. But he couldn't stop himself. He wanted to forget everything, pick her up and take her to his bed. Worry only about pleasing her and losing himself in her body.

He forced himself to end the kiss, but he couldn't release her hand, he couldn't turn away. He hadn't felt this strongly about a woman in a long time…no, he'd *never* felt this. And although Callie's answer might mean he could trust her, he still wasn't sure he could trust his feelings.

"We need to hurry," he managed to say, his voice gruff with the longing pulsing through his blood.

She nodded, but she didn't move, as if he had seized her heart as powerfully as she had his.

Pulling in a sharp breath, he tore his gaze from hers and stepped to the door before he did something stupid like kiss her again. Or make love to her.

Or just flat-out give her his heart.

Since Fahad acted as Efraim's personal bodyguard as well as the head of all security arrangements for Efraim and the rest of the royals, both he and Efraim had kept the doors adjoining each other's rooms unlocked, in case a hurried entry was necessary. The doors for his side and Fahad's side opened easily under his hand, and he and Callie slipped into the next room.

Whereas Efraim had a suite, Fahad had only a single spacious room. A king-size bed dominated the space. The rest of the usual furniture—bureau, desk, leather chair—rimmed the edges. It was a nice space, although Fahad typically spent so little time in his room, Efraim doubted he noticed.

"What are we looking for?" Callie asked. She opened the closet door.

"I don't know. Anything…unusual."

Efraim started with the bureau drawers. Fahad was very organized. One drawer held clothing that didn't belong hung in the closet. The next a collection of holsters designed to conceal a handgun under various types of clothing. He didn't see anything out of place, anything that raised red flags. He glanced up at Callie. "Find anything?"

"Just traditional robes, business suits, a Kevlar vest and a rifle case. I assume the latter is for the weapon he had with him." She knelt down. "And there's the room safe."

He slid the drawer holding the holsters shut. "He probably has a few handguns in there. Some ammunition."

"Any idea of the combo?"

He scoured his brain. The combination was probably something he should know, but he couldn't come up with anything. He'd left so much to Fahad, not just his personal security but the complex problems of coordinating details with the other COIN leaders, the intricacies of travel arrangements and a host of other problems. Fahad had dealt with it all, freeing Efraim to focus on governing Nadar and foreign relations.

But that was all over now. And Efraim had no idea who he could trust. Kateb was next in line for the position. But Fahad's younger brother nursed an underlying anger and fundamentalist views that reminded Efraim too much of his own younger brother for comfort. He had only to think of the way Kateb had treated Callie to feel uncomfortable about the man all over again. He would never turn over decision-making power to Kateb.

Again a current of loss flowed through him.

"Any ideas?"

He glanced up at Callie's voice and brought his focus back to the safe's combination. "I'm sorry, no."

She sat on one hip, slinging her blue-jeaned legs to one side. "I'll see what I can figure out."

He let Callie handle the safe and moved to the laptop sitting on the desk. Now here was something he knew a bit about.

He fired it up and grabbed a flash drive from the laptop case sitting on the floor. After plugging in the flash drive, he started copying Fahad's files. Maybe among the schedules and security strategies would be a detail that would shed new light on things.

He wasn't sure how much time had passed when the sound of a voice came from the hall outside the door.

The sheriff was on his way.

Callie focused wide eyes on him. "We'd better get out of here." Abandoning the still-locked safe, she scrambled to her feet and closed the closet door.

Efraim stared at the screen, willing the computer to copy files faster.

The voices grew louder.

"Efraim. Hurry. They're coming."

He pulled out the flash drive and stuck it in his pocket. He turned off the computer. He wasn't sure if it would look more suspicious to leave it open or turn it off without letting it shut the programs down properly. In the end, it probably didn't matter. Any decent computer specialist would be able to see the device was turned on after Fahad's death.

And it wouldn't take much on the sheriff's part to figure out the culprit was him.

He stood, about to leave the screen open, when the top of the hotel desk caught his attention. A smattering of American coins scattered the desk along with a cell phone the size of a credit card and a wad of receipts and a matchbook. He pocketed the phone and receipts and looked at the matchbook. Fahad hadn't left the resort since the night of the car bomb. At least not that Efraim knew. Yet the matchbook on the desk was emblazoned with the logo and address of a local tavern in Dumont.

One he had not visited when out with Efraim.

"Hurry." Callie stood in the connecting doorway, both portals wide open.

Before he stuffed the matchbook in his pocket along with the rest, something else caught his eye. Inside the matchbook's flap, he spied the name Tanya and a number, written in a woman's hand.

Maybe they'd found something interesting after all.

"WHAT DID YOU find?" Safe in Efraim's room with the connecting door locked, Callie focused on the papers in his hand and tried to calm the tremble that claimed every nerve in her body. She didn't like any of this, yet she'd promised Efraim she'd go along. She couldn't back out, even now that he'd stolen possible evidence right out from under Jake Wolf's nose.

If she were honest with herself, she needed to know the truth, almost as much as Efraim. Only partially for Fahad's sake—she could still hear his bitter words ringing in her head, words she didn't have the heart to repeat for Efraim. But Efraim's insistence in the boardroom that the man who attacked him was a local made her uneasy. She had to know if it was true.

Efraim pulled a collection of paper out of his pocket and spilled it all onto the desk in the sitting room of his suite. He worriedly sorted through the mess. The sound of voices hummed from the room next door. "Most of these receipts are from the first night we were here. The night we all had dinner in Dumont."

Also the night of the car bomb and Amir's disappearance, but she let that go unsaid. "And the rest?"

"It looks like Fahad found his way into Dumont the last few nights." His voice dipped, tension ringing in each word.

"He didn't tell you he was going?"

"I didn't have a clue. And things weren't settled enough around here or safe enough for my head of security—the man in charge of coordinating security for all of us—to be running into town for no reason."

"How many times did he go to Dumont?"

"Twice since the explosion."

"And you think it might have something to do with his death?"

"It was an American who attacked me. A local. It made me think. What if I wasn't the primary target? What if Fahad was?"

"You think that's possible?" Callie asked.

"I think we have to consider every angle."

She tried to do just that. A cold chill ran down her spine. "You think he might have run into some of the protestors? Made one of them angry enough to kill him?"

"It's possible."

"There has to be more behind Fahad's murder than a chance run-in with a frightened local." At least she hoped so. But she had no clue what circumstances would make any of this easier. "Do you know why he went to Dumont in the first place?"

"I don't know, but I have a guess." He held a match-book scissored between index and middle finger.

Callie recognized the logo of the Tumbledown Tavern. "He went to a bar? There's a bar here at the lodge."

"He didn't necessarily go to get a drink." He flipped open the flap and handed the matches to her.

When she saw the name and number, Efraim's line of thought became clear. "A woman. He went to meet a woman."

"And maybe a local man wasn't happy about it."

Deciding that neither of them could sleep despite the late hour and that Efraim preferred to not sit around in his suite waiting for the sheriff's questions, the two of them made their way back out to the pickup and were soon back on the road to town. At least during the tourist season, the bar should still be hopping until closing time.

The town of Dumont boasted a population of less than seven thousand, not including the surrounding ranches, like the Seven M. But this time of year, tourists flooded into town like water gushing out of the mountains during spring thaw. Located at the foot of the Wind River Mountains, travelers came for hiking, camping, fishing, climbing and mountaineering. Some traveled on to Grand Teton National Park and Yellowstone. But some ended up at guest ranches, luxury accommodations like the Wind River Ranch and Resort and more modest operations like the half-dozen others in the area.

And when nighttime fell, vacationers and locals alike enjoyed the summer nightlife in Dumont.

The parking lot of the Tumbledown Tavern was packed with everything from motorcycles to cars to pickups dirtier than Russ's. They wound through the lot, finally finding a vacant space in the gravel lot in the back. They circled the building on foot. The smell of fried food, thunk of drums and whine of a guitar floated on cool night air. A sign out front heralded a country-and-rock band called The Unforgiven that had traveled from Cody to put on tonight's show.

A burly local wearing a cowboy hat and boots stood outside the door. He crossed his arms and scrutinized the driver's licenses of a group of girls wearing ribbons braided into their hair.

Efraim's steps slowed. He stopped before they reached the lighted area around the entrance. "See his shirt?"

She focused on the cotton T-shirt stretched across his chest. It looked homemade, a white shirt with iron-on letters. But slick or not, the message was clear.

ROYALS GO HOME

An ache settled in Callie's stomach. She looked past the bouncer and into the bar. Three more men just inside the door sported similar shirts, some more derogatory than the message worn by the bouncer.

"This is just…surreal." A weight settled into Callie's stomach, making her queasiness grow. "Some of these people…I don't understand it. They're the nicest people you'd ever want to meet. Generous, you know? They'd do anything to help a neighbor."

"But not to help a foreigner."

She shook her head. Before seeing this scene, before witnessing her own father's and brothers' behavior, she would have disagreed with Efraim's statement. These were good people. They'd always been generous in the past. And tolerant, even of those different from themselves. But now?

What was happening to her country? Her town? Her family? Was everyone so driven by hate that they couldn't see what they were becoming? "They're better than this."

Efraim nodded. "I've seen it in my countrymen, too. Neighbor turning against neighbor."

It's what they'd talked about in the boardroom, what she'd heard in Fahad's voice and seen in Kateb's eyes, and once again, she had to agree. It was rude, cruel and maybe much worse. Fear made people do desperate things, she knew. It made them cross lines they never otherwise would even consider crossing. "You'd better let me nose around this crowd on my own."

For a second, he looked as if he was about to argue, then he squinted into the bar. "You're right. I have a phone call to make anyway."

She opened her mouth, then clamped down on the inside of her bottom lip. It wasn't any of her business who he was planning to call. "Okay. Here." She held out the set of truck keys dangling from a fob sporting the Wyoming-cowboy-on-a-bucking-bronc logo.

He took the key chain, turned and strode back across the parking lot. She hesitated, then ran to catch up.

"What is it?"

He looked good in the crisp white button-down shirt and black trousers. Too good. He'd stand out, even just sitting in the truck making a phone call. She didn't know why she hadn't thought about it before they'd approached the bar, but at least she'd thought of it now. "I have an idea."

She waited while he opened the truck door. Then she leaned in. Stretching over the seat, she groped in a box, her fingers touching stiff felt.

She pulled out Russ's new Stetson and handed it to Efraim. "Try it on."

He fitted the cowboy hat on his head. The beige-silver color of the hat looked striking against his nearly black hair.

She shook her head. "And here I was hoping it would make you stand out less."

He gave her a smile that made her bones feel soft.

She wanted him to kiss her again, to forget all about murder and fear and oil leases. She wanted to head back to the luxurious bed in his suite and stay there forever, wrapped in his arms.

She looked down at the gravel under her boots. "Okay, then, I'll just be a few minutes. If I find Tanya, I'll let you know." She forced her feet to turn and carry her away from the pickup.

She retraced her steps across the parking lot, gravel crunching under her boots. She didn't know what it was about that man, but just being near him made her feel as light-headed as if she'd downed a whole six-pack on her own. She needed to keep her head clear, not full of fantasies about a man who could never accept both of her worlds. A man who one of those worlds would never accept.

She stepped through the door and into a haze of smoke. The dance floor was packed with people, some dancing, some standing and watching the band, beers in their fists.

Callie checked her watch. Almost bar time. She didn't have a lot of time to find a woman named Tanya in a crowd like this.

She scanned the room. If the man who shot Fahad was one of those cowboys wearing the homemade T-shirts, she doubted he'd be able to keep his mouth shut about it. In the current atmosphere, he was certain to be hailed a hero. And as the cowboys raised their beers in a toast, she had to wonder what they were drinking to.

Maybe once she tracked down this Tanya, she could find someone to fill her in on the latest gossip.

"Cal. I was wondering where you hurried off to."

She turned toward the familiar voice and met eyes as blue as her own. "Brent." Her gaze only had to lower a little to read the iron-on letters on the shirt stretched across her big brother's chest.

Chapter Nine

Callie thought she'd been upset by the ugly spectacle of the mob protest before. Now, looking up at her oldest brother, she felt more than a little sick. "How can you be a part of something like this, Brent? What are you doing here?"

"What are *you* doing here with *him?*" Brent asked.

She let out an exasperated breath. He must have seen her with Efraim before they returned to the truck. "I work for the Office of Foreign Affairs."

"You can't tell me that's business."

"No, it's also about finding a murderer."

"Murderer? Suddenly protecting your own is murder?" He glared at her out of the corner of his eye and took a swig of beer. "That sheik, he and his friends are no good, Callie. You have to see that."

"I see a brother I'd hoped was better than this." She shot a look at the T-shirt.

"Give me a break. This was a peaceful town until they got here. No explosions. No murders. Your royal friends have turned Dumont into a war zone. We just want our town back, our peaceful way of life."

"I'd love to believe that you want peace, but if that's

really the case, threatening and violence isn't a way to get there."

"Who's threatening? Who's committing violence?"

"Whoever set off that car bomb. Whoever shot Fahad Bahir."

"What makes you think it was someone from Dumont?"

She would like to believe it wasn't. She was desperate to believe that. But she couldn't close her eyes and avoid what was right in front of her. "Oh, I don't know. Maybe because there's enough hate in the air around here to choke a horse."

"If your royal pals don't like that, they should go home. They're in our country. They don't belong here."

"And it's exactly that type of attitude that might lead someone to start shooting."

"Are you accusing me of murder, little sis?"

Was she? She had to admit that of all her brothers, Brent was the one who was bitter. Brent was the one struggling to control his anger. Brent's life had changed in the Middle East and it would never be the same again. But with all of Brent's challenges, she still couldn't accept the thought of him shooting Fahad in cold blood and attacking Efraim. Maybe she was just closing her eyes to reality, but she couldn't believe her brother was a murderer. "Of course not."

"Good. Because if I'd wanted these foreigners dead, not only would this Fahad be in the morgue, your friend in the truck would be with him."

She'd always been able to handle Brent when they were growing up. She knew her brother was having trouble adjusting to the unexpected turn his life had taken. She knew he'd seen horrible things in Afghanistan, and those things had changed him. But she couldn't stand here and listen to him talk of killing Efraim.

She pushed past him.

"Cal."

She kept going, wading farther into the crowd. She needed to get away from Brent before she belted him. Before she lost all hope that the decent streak he used to possess had been killed right along with his military career.

A hand closed around her biceps. "Callie, stop."

She wrenched her arm free from her brother's grip and tried to keep pushing through the crowd.

"Where are you going?" He grabbed her again, this time his grip too strong to break. "Callie?"

She turned and looked up at her big brother. She'd always looked up to him, ever since she could remember. But after his threat, she had trouble doing so now. "I have things to take care of."

"What things?"

She shook her head.

"Listen, I went too far back there."

"Really? You think a death threat is too far?" All her life she'd been a peacemaker. God knew, she'd gained most of that experience making peace between Brent and Joe when they were growing up. But this day had been too long, too traumatic and too filled with hate and violence. She'd reached her limit. "The men at the Wind River Ranch and Resort are not our enemies."

"How do you know that?"

"I know."

He shook his head. "I don't think you're seeing things straight."

"I *know* you're not. What do you want, Brent? What does this crowd want? A lynching? Do they want to kill the outsider? Fear what they don't understand? Destroy it? You're better than that. We Americans, we're all better than that."

"You haven't seen what I've seen, Callie."

"No, I haven't. But you haven't seen what I've seen either. We can move beyond all this hate and fear. We can work together."

"My sister the dreamer." He gave her an apologetic quirk of the lips.

She wasn't sure she still had the capacity to accept the apology. She turned away from him, ready to head into the crowd.

"Callie, wait."

She paused. Brent was infuriating and bitter and impossible, but he was still her brother. "What?"

"Why are you here?"

"I'm looking for a woman named Tanya."

"Tanya? Tanya what?"

"I don't know her last name." She pulled the matchbook out of her jeans pocket and gave it to him.

He squinted at the writing in the dim light. "That would be Tanya Driscoll. Why are you looking for her?"

"You know her?"

"Not really. But Russ does."

"Russ? How?"

"About two weeks ago, she gave him one of these." He handed the matchbook back to her.

"And he called her?"

"You know Russ."

She did. Out of all her good-looking brothers, Russ had the most luck with women. It had been that way since grade school. And he enjoyed it for all it was worth. "Two weeks ago? Are you sure?"

"I'm sure. We were here for my birthday. Russ, Joe and me."

"How many times did he go out with her?"

"I don't know. Three, four times maybe. Why? What's so interesting about this Tanya?"

"That's what I'm trying to figure out." And she didn't like where her thoughts were leading. Three or four dates with the same woman was a lot for her little brother. "Did Russ really like her?"

"He sure talks about her enough." Brent shrugged. "She's hot."

Apparently hot enough for both Russ and Fahad to want to spend time with her. And that worried Callie. Brent was a bitter, angry man besides being a natural hothead. Russ took after his oldest brother in every way, even hoping to follow in his military career footsteps until Brent's injury had changed everyone's plans. Now he had almost graduated from college and was adrift, with no future in mind except ranching and chasing women and, like Brent, always spoiling for a fight.

Could Russ…

She shook her head, trying to dislodge the thought. She'd come into the Tumbledown Tavern to find Tanya, and that's what she needed to do, not let her imagination run amok before she had a single fact.

"How about a peace offering? What can I get you,

Cal?" Brent asked, motioning to the bartender by raising his empty glass.

"Nothing, thanks." She scanned the crowd, then looked up at her brother. "On second thought, you can point out Tanya Driscoll."

"Love to. Only she's not here tonight."

Callie let out a breath. Maybe it was just as well. It was late. She was bone-tired, the adrenaline of all they'd weathered today was finally wearing off. Maybe it was best to just drop Efraim off at the Wind River Ranch and Resort and go to bed.

For a second the image of the luxurious bed in Efraim's room skipped into her mind. She pushed it away, trying not to think about how horrified her brother would be if he had the slightest idea what she'd just been picturing. "I'll see you at home, then."

"Wait, Callie. I said she's not here, but I know where you can probably find her."

As soon as Callie's cute little blue-jeaned butt had swayed across the parking lot, Efraim pulled out his cell phone. It would be morning in Saruk. He hoped Darek wouldn't be attending a state function of some kind and unable to talk.

He pulled up Darek's private cell number and hit Dial. He still couldn't quite believe he'd agreed to stick around and give COIN a chance. It was Callie. Between her smile and his hormones, she could probably talk him into anything. He had to be careful where she was concerned.

Exactly why he needed another perspective.

"Efraim." Darek's voice sounded clear, as if he

was sitting right there in the pickup. "Have you found Amir?"

"No. No sign of him yet."

"I am sorry."

"Thank you. But Amir is not the reason I called." Darek had a clear head about political matters and had always been a good sounding board for Efraim. "Can you talk?"

"I have to leave in a few minutes. Until then, my time is yours."

"You remember my cousin, Fahad Bahir?"

"He is in charge of security?"

Was. Efraim swallowed, his throat aching. "He was killed. Shot." He didn't go into the rest. Whether he was the target or Fahad, it didn't matter. It would all be the same to Darek.

Darek's heavy sigh shuddered over the phone. "Get out of there, Efraim."

Exactly the reaction Efraim expected. "I can't."

"You can. We can come up with an agreement over the oil leases on our own. We don't need the Americans."

It wasn't that easy and Darek knew it. "And if we cut the Americans out, who will the oil go through?"

"My father has contacts in Russia. We keep the oil here. In our hemisphere. You of all people should know we can't trust the Americans."

He did know. It was only when he was around Callie that he wanted to forget. "The Americans' offer is more favorable to us. Stefan Lutece, Sebastian and Antoine, Amir, that's why we are here. That's why you should be here, too."

"My father won't have anything to do with the

Americans. If your father still had the heart to understand what was going on, he wouldn't either."

Efraim knew he was right. After the disastrous treaty his father signed years ago, he'd distanced himself from negotiations of any kind. All but the ceremonial aspects of leading Nadar were Efraim's responsibility now. A responsibility that most of the time felt like a yoke around his neck.

"Fahad called me."

Darek's words jolted through his body like an electric shock. "When?"

"Yesterday. He was concerned about you."

"Concerned?" He thought of the argument they'd had before Efraim had Kateb trailer a horse out to the badlands for him. Before Fahad had followed him and gotten shot. "Why was he concerned?"

"He wanted me to talk some sense into you."

Efraim gritted his teeth. "It was about searching for Amir, wasn't it?"

"No."

"Then what?"

"A woman. A blonde who works for the United States government. Fahad was concerned about her."

The second surprise Darek had dealt him in the last minute. "Callie McGuire?"

"I know this is delicate. I'm sorry. I told him there was nothing to worry about. That you would never let a mere woman sway you from doing what you felt was right for your country, let alone an American woman who will profit more than anyone if this oil deal goes through."

"What did Fahad say?" He wasn't sure why he wanted

to know. What good would it do? Fahad was dead. And Callie…he knew she wasn't trying to manipulate him.

"Just that this woman was doing all she could to get close to you."

He pressed back another surge of anger. He couldn't stand the thought of anyone talking about Callie this way. And about him, as if he was being led around like a dog.

"Whenever he turned around, he said she was there, trying to catch your eye."

Efraim thought of Callie riding toward him on the BLM. He'd thought it was unusual she'd come after him. At least he had before he'd learned it was Stefan who had sent her. But not for a moment did he feel as though Callie was trying to manipulate him. No, she wouldn't.

"He was concerned she would…"

"Would what?"

"Find her way into your bed. Take unfair advantage to see that this agreement of hers went through."

He shook his head. He'd known Fahad had as many reservations about COIN as he had. No, probably more. But for him to insult Callie this way… It was good that Efraim hadn't known about his call to Darek until now.

"There is no danger, Darek. If I choose to remain part of COIN, I will do so of my own free will."

"That's what I told Fahad. Who knows? Maybe he was jealous. He said she was quite beautiful. He always liked blondes."

Efraim gritted his teeth at the thought of Fahad or any man coming on to Callie. "Yes, maybe that's it."

"May he have many blondes waiting for him in

heaven," Darek said. "I have to go, Efraim. Please call when Amir is found, if not before."

"I will. And thank you, Darek."

"For what?"

"For helping me gain some perspective, as always." Efraim ended the call just as he caught sight of Callie striding toward the truck, blond hair fanning out behind her in the gentle night wind.

She climbed into the driver's seat, a small smile on her face.

A smile that gave Efraim a warm shiver.

Darek wasn't right about Callie, but that didn't mean Efraim didn't have to be careful. Her effect on him seemed to grow with each minute they spent together. "You found this Tanya?"

"No, but I have a full name and a place to look."

He returned her smile, although his felt like it lighted his whole face. He was ready to get some answers or at least narrow down the possibilities. "Then let's go."

Callie drove a few blocks out to the edge of town and turned into the parking lot of a late-night diner. "Tanya Driscoll works here. Brent says if she isn't at the Tumbledown, she's probably working."

"Brent? Your brother?"

She nodded, but offered no more.

"He knows her?"

"He knows *of* her. Says she moved to town about two weeks ago."

"Just before we arrived for the summit."

"Right around the time we finalized the plans."

The parking lot was less than half-full, late-night diners who left the bars early, no doubt. She swung the truck into an empty space and switched off the engine. "Not that we know the timing is related."

"You think her arrival is just a coincidence?"

"I didn't say that. I just think we need to know more before we jump to conclusions."

"Then let's hope Tanya can give us more."

They got out of the pickup and made their way into the diner. A smattering of customers sat at the tables, chatting a little too loudly and smothering their night's drinking with burgers and breakfast foods. Silverware rolled in paper napkins perched on empty tables, waiting for the night's rush at closing time. In a town the size of Dumont, this must be the only twenty-four-hour diner, the place to go for the after-bar crowd.

Efraim and Callie stopped at the hostess stand and waited for a man wearing a crumpled dress shirt to look up from a laminated sheet mapping all the tables in the restaurant. Efraim peered at the sheet, taking in the black marker splitting the tables into two sections, the names scrawled in the middle of each.

"Excuse me," Callie said. "We were wondering—"

"Can we sit in Tanya's section?" Efraim interrupted.

Callie looked up at him with arched brows.

"Tanya. Sure." The man scooped up two menus printed on a single sheet of laminated paper. He drew an X through one of the squares representing tables on the chart and motioned them to follow.

He stopped at a window booth, set the menus on the table and left.

Callie slid into one side of the booth. Efraim took the other. She picked up the menu. "Hungry?"

He realized for the first time that he hadn't eaten all day. "Actually, yes."

"Might as well order. Maybe she'll be more forthcoming if there's the promise of a tip in the balance."

Efraim spotted the woman who must be Tanya long before she reached their table. She was a good-looking girl, medium brown hair that curled seductively around her shoulders. She wore a white shirt like the man at the desk, but hers was unbuttoned low enough to earn her some extra tips. An apron pulled tight around her hips outlining her slim body as effectively as a slinky dress.

She stood in the doorway to the kitchen, talking to someone they couldn't see. Her lips moved quickly and her body leaned forward, as if she was telling someone something urgent. She was too far away for him to hear what she was saying, but something struck him as out of place.

Finally she scurried into the dining room with a tray of food. She stopped at a nearby table and delivered the plates, then moved to a table of four men who'd just taken their seats, their voices loud and faces flushed from a night of drinking. At least they weren't wearing T-shirts telling Efraim and "his kind" to go home.

Small favors.

Having finished flirting with the men, Tanya reached their table, order pad in hand. She turned a smile on them so brilliant and perfect that it looked as if it were made of plastic like a Barbie doll. "So what can I get the two of you tonight?"

They ordered a couple of burgers with fries and the works. Tanya thanked them and was about to turn away when Callie gave the woman a big smile. "You're Tanya. Tanya Driscoll. Right?"

The false smile fell from Tanya's lips. "Yeah. So?"

"You hang out at the Tumbledown Tavern?"

"Sometimes."

"Nearly every night you aren't working is what I hear."

Her frown deepened. Without the smile, Tanya looked older, harder. And there was something about her that bothered Efraim, like what he'd felt while watching her earlier. Something wasn't right. If only he could figure out what it was.

She glanced toward the kitchen as if plotting her getaway. "So I like to party. What of it?"

"Nothing." Efraim gave a little chuckle. "We were just wondering if you knew a friend of ours."

"A friend? Who?"

"A cousin." He pulled the matchbook from his pocket and held it up to her. "You gave this to him. Fahad Bahir."

She didn't bother to look at the matchbook. "So? He's not married or anything, is he? If he is, I didn't know about it."

Efraim didn't answer. There was something about Tanya's casual quip that wasn't exactly off the cuff. He wasn't sure he could put his finger on it, but something felt rehearsed in her speech. As if she was trying very hard to seem nonchalant.

"So you wanted him to call you?" Callie prompted.

"Sure. Men like me. So what? Is that a crime?" She focused on Callie, as if her questions might be simple jealousy talking.

Efraim wanted to laugh. As far as he was concerned this woman should be the jealous one. Everything about Callie felt so sincere, so candid. But Tanya? Even her candidness felt false and forced. "Did Fahad call you?"

"No. But I saw him at the bar. And afterward." She smiled at Efraim, not taunting, but inviting.

"Did he know that you were also seeing other men?" Callie asked.

Efraim narrowed his eyes on her, unsure who she was talking about.

"I don't know. Maybe. It was not as if he gave me a ring."

Efraim didn't want to ask the question, but he had to. "Were you seeing anyone else who is staying at the Wind River Ranch?"

"Men have money. They want to spend it on me. I'm not going to say no."

He would take that as a yes. "Who?"

She shrugged, as if it was all horribly unimportant. "Cute man from a country called Nadar."

"Fahad was from Nadar," Callie said, frowning.

Tanya rolled her eyes. "Not Fahad. He was cheap. He only bought drinks. This other one..." She smiled. Her hand rose to a beautiful stone pendant on a chain around her neck. "He knew how to treat a lady."

The back of Efraim's neck prickled. "The generous one, what was his name?"

"It started with a *K*. I think it was something like..."

A weight descended on Efraim's chest. He didn't know how this piece fit in a puzzle about an American shooting Fahad, but it gave him a deep feeling of dread all the same. "Kateb."

Tanya smiled. "That's right. Kateb."

Chapter Ten

Callie and Efraim sat and wolfed down their burgers in silence. But even as hungry as she was, Callie knew their lack of conversation wasn't caused by their need to eat. It wasn't even caused by the shocker Tanya had delivered and the need for both of them to let it sink in.

From the moment Tanya had uttered Kateb's name, Callie knew she'd made a big mistake in not telling Efraim her brother, too, had dated their waitress. She hadn't done it for the simple reason that she'd known he would take that as proof that Russ had shot Fahad. And that she was afraid of the consequences, whether it was true or not. The consequences for the bond that was growing between them. The consequences for her own dreams about what could possibly be.

Stupid.

She dug into her burger, not even able to taste the meat and bun and cheddar cheese.

Efraim was first to break the silence. "I'm afraid I might owe you an apology."

"You don't."

"No, I thought the man who shot Fahad was American because of his voice. Maybe I was wrong."

She shook her head. There was more. More Efraim didn't know. "I found out something else at the tavern."

"Something about Kateb?"

"No."

"I thought he was acting strange when we returned to the resort tonight."

She shook her head. She didn't know if Kateb had something to hide, if what Efraim obviously feared was true. But she knew he didn't have all the facts. And when she told him the rest, she had the feeling he wouldn't be happy. She had to figure out how to soften the blow. "You can't be too hard on Kateb. Grief affects people differently. None of us know how we'd react to news of our brother's death."

"That might be true. But Fahad and Kateb, they weren't close. They were like me and my brother. They shared blood, but they didn't always see eye to eye."

"I often don't see eye to eye with my brothers." An understatement, especially lately.

"But you are not rivals with them."

"This has happened before with women?"

"Women. Cars. Homes. Guns. You name it. Kateb is always trying to outdo Fahad. And more often than not, he fails."

"Then he should be used to it, right?"

"Not Kateb. I think the rivalry made him hate his brother. And I think Fahad enjoyed egging him on."

Callie's mind scrambled to catch up. "But you said the man who jumped you had an American accent."

"Kateb went to school here in America."

"But his accent—he doesn't sound like a local."

"No. Not now. Now he is used to living in Nadar. Working in Nadar. He has reverted to his original accent. But he is still able to speak like an American. He does it often for fun, like a parlor trick. He's very good at it."

"And you don't think you would have recognized his voice?"

He shrugged a shoulder. "He could have disguised it. I was not expecting to know the voice. And now that I think back, it could have sounded like him."

She shook her head. "I don't know. I suppose it's possible, but I think there are other explanations."

"Like what?"

That was her opening. She needed to tell him.

She set the rest of her burger down on the plate. Her stomach felt like it was being squeezed by a strong hand. She never should have eaten something so heavy, so fast. She hoped to God she wasn't going to be sick. "Like the Russian mob." She choked down the nausea with disappointment in herself. She'd taken the easy way. She'd had the perfect opportunity to bring up Russ's history with Tanya, and she ducked out.

Efraim stared at her, as if something she said had changed his whole way of thinking.

Or was it something she *hadn't* said?

She shook her head. Efraim had no way of knowing that her brother had also dated the ever-popular Tanya. No way of knowing that he was just the type of hothead who might take offense to a man like Fahad horning in on his territory. Callie didn't believe Russ would shoot Fahad, kill him in cold blood. There was no way. But she needed to tell Efraim nonetheless. She'd worked too hard to win his trust to keep anything like that from him now.

She was just afraid of what he'd do, what he'd think, once he knew. What he'd think about Russ.

And what he'd think about her.

She pulled in a deep breath and pushed ahead. "There's more. I also—"

Efraim held up a hand to stop her. "Russian. That's it."

"The Russian mob?" She frowned. They'd talked about the sniper who'd attacked Stefan and Jane. They'd discussed the possibility that the mob wanted to stop the COIN summit. That they'd sent the sniper to do just that. That they might have planted the bomb. Or shot Fahad. This was common knowledge they'd discussed many times.

So why was Efraim acting like it was some big revelation? "I'm sorry, Efraim. I'm not following."

"Tanya. Before she came to take our order, she was standing in the kitchen doorway talking to someone, someone I couldn't see."

Callie glanced at the kitchen entrance behind her. No one was milling there now. "What did she say?"

"I don't know. I couldn't hear anything from this distance. But something about the conversation seemed strange to me. I couldn't figure out what. Until now." His dark eyes gleamed with whatever he'd discovered.

Callie leaned forward, arms on either side of her plate. "What was it?"

"Russian."

She shook her head. That was what he'd said before, and she still wasn't following.

"The language," he explained. "Tanya and who-ever is in the kitchen were speaking to each other in Russian."

A frisson of fear shot up Callie's spine. "You think she might be working for the Russian mob?"

Efraim gave a shrug, but the curve of his lips told her that that was exactly what he was thinking. "Maybe our little waitress doesn't like to party as much as she says. Maybe she's interested in something else entirely."

HIS REALIZATION having quashed both his and Callie's appetites, Efraim threw some American dollars on the table for a tip and stepped up to the cashier to pay their bill. Tanya seemed to have vanished after they'd grilled her, never filling their water or coffee, never returning to the neighboring tables, never even poking her head out of the kitchen.

Callie shifted her feet on the low-pile carpet and scanned the restaurant. "Did everyone leave? Where's the host who seated us?"

Other diners craned their necks, as if wondering the same thing.

Efraim peeled a couple of twenties from his wallet and plopped them on the seating chart. "That should be more than enough."

Callie looked at the money. "I'll say."

He moved a hand behind her back and ushered her to the door. "We have to get out of here."

"Do you think they know we've figured something out? Is that why everyone has disappeared?"

"I don't know. But I don't want to wait to find out." They had to get back to the Wind River Ranch and

Resort. They would be safe there, and they needed to tell the other royals about this latest development. Who knew what other men in their entourages had fallen under Tanya's spell? Who knew what information Fahad or Kateb might have unwittingly given away? They had to circle the wagons, as the Americans said, and figure out what to do next.

Kateb. He needed to talk to Kateb most of all. Efraim felt a headache coming on at the thought of the two brothers fighting over a woman who'd been playing them the entire time. How ironic that Fahad had voiced his doubts about Callie to Darek when all the while, he was flirting with a woman who wanted to see all of them dead.

And who was actively trying to make it happen.

The parking lot was full of cars, but no voices, no people. Except for the crowd inside the diner, the town felt as if it was shutting down for the night. Somewhere in the darkness, a coyote howled.

They circled the diner heading toward the back lot where they'd left the truck. As soon as they'd rounded the corner, Efraim slowed.

When they'd arrived, two lights had illuminated the back lot, a streetlight and a light perched on the diner's back wall. Now both of them were dark.

A scan of the lot and he knew why.

Shadows loitered near the pickup. Two men. Their arms hung by their sides. Efraim couldn't see their hands, but he guessed they weren't empty.

Efraim grasped Callie's elbow and pulled her to the side of the building.

She turned to him with wide eyes. "Do you think they're—"

"Yes."

They both reached for their cell phones. She unclipped hers first.

"Who are you calling?"

"911."

"Not police." He covered her phone and hand with his. He wasn't sure if the men had seen them or not, but he didn't want to take the chance. If they were with the Russian mob, as he suspected, they would have guns. They wouldn't hesitate to kill. He needed to get Callie out of here. He needed to make sure she was safe.

And he didn't trust the police to save them.

"Run back inside the diner. Call the Wind River Ranch. Tell the others. Ask them to send help."

"A deputy can get here faster."

"I'm not so sure about that." He glanced around the edge of the building. The men hadn't moved. Maybe they hadn't spotted Callie and him. Yet. But that didn't give them the time to argue. "Just do it, Callie. Trust me."

She nodded and turned.

He could hear her footsteps scampering away fast, but he kept his eyes on the shadows.

They were waiting for him, that was certain. Tanya must have called in the muscle. But how, in a parking lot half-full of pickups, did these men know that particular truck was theirs?

He pressed against the building's siding, the corrugated steel cool through his shirt's thin fabric. He was painfully aware of the lack of weight around his waist, on his hip. The sheriff had ultimately taken his gun from Callie when one of her brothers had helpfully pointed out it wasn't hers. He was unarmed. And odds were, the men waiting for him weren't.

He could have helped himself to one of Fahad's pistols, if they'd been able to open the safe. Or he could have gotten a weapon from Kateb or one of his other men. Why had he assumed a trip to town would be safe? He should have thought ahead.

He scanned the parking lot, looking for a way to slip around the men. In this area, without a vehicle, they wouldn't get far. His eye caught on the tall grizzly fence surrounding the Dumpster. Seven feet high and rimmed with razor wire, he couldn't climb it, but it could provide cover. Allow him to move closer to the men.

And then what?

He needed a weapon. He glanced around the side and back of the diner. Only a few blades of brown grass poking up in the space between pavement and siding. Yet…he spotted something glistening in the front parking lot lights.

A beer bottle.

Great, between that and the Dumpster, he had a lot of nothing against two guns. They had to wait for men from the ranch.

And if those two men got tired of waiting and decided to come collect them from the diner?

If these two shadows were mobsters, it was him they wanted dead. Him they would target to stop the COIN compact. As long as Callie wasn't with him, she'd be safe.

A footfall sounded behind him.

He brought up his hands, spun around.

Callie stopped, breathing heavy. "An armed man was in front of the diner. Like he was waiting. Tanya was with him."

Efraim muttered a curse under his breath. "Did he see you?"

"I don't think so. He didn't follow."

"Did you get a chance to call?"

"Sebastian said they'd send help." Her gaze slanted to the side. "I called 911, too. To hedge our bets."

He thought of the corruption Stefan had encountered in the ranks of law enforcement. He didn't believe Sheriff Wolf was corrupt, but the man obviously didn't trust Efraim. And even if he was pure as the snow on the mountaintops, that didn't mean his deputies weren't on the take.

He supposed they'd deal with that if they had to. "Sebastian will handle things, but it doesn't hurt to have a backup plan."

"So what do we do now?"

"We wait."

"Here?"

"No. Too dangerous."

"We can't go around front," Callie said.

"All that's left is one side or the other." He scanned the area. A gas station was next to the diner on one side, then a smattering of what appeared to be tourist shops in a long strip mall. On the other, the land dipped sharply to a creek bed, then climbed to a budget motel. If they could reach the creek, maybe they could follow it under the highway. Maybe they could find something on the other side, at least a place to hide until help arrived. "How deep is that creek?"

"It varies, depending on how much snow is melting in the mountains. It's pretty wide on this side of the highway, though. We shouldn't have to swim."

Not ideal. Maybe he could find—

"They're coming." Callie's voice was only a whisper, but it rang with alarm.

He snapped his eyes to the shadows. They were moving. Not urgently, but purposefully.

A voice sounded behind them, toward the front of the building. A man's voice speaking in Russian.

Efraim wasn't going to stay to hear what he had to say. They were out of options. "I'm going to distract them. When I signal, run for the creek."

He could see the fear in her eyes. She set her chin, her nod calm, resolute.

She really was something.

"And keep your head low."

He reached down and picked up the empty beer bottle he'd noticed earlier. The glass felt cold and slick in his hand. He eyed the grizzly fence. He had only one shot at this. It had to work. He needed to buy time.

The men kept coming, searching between and inside cars on their approach.

He could feel Callie tense beside him. "Yes."

"As soon as it hits, we run." He drew his arm back and let the beer bottle fly.

He didn't wait to see if it had cleared the tall fence, but he heard it hit something hard and shatter.

They raced across the gravel and plunged down the steep bank. His heart pounded against his rib cage. Next to him, he could hear Callie gasp as she skidded, then caught herself before she fell.

He reached out and grasped her hand. The soft earth crumbled under their feet. They slid down the bank, half running, half skidding as if on skis. The black, glistening stretch of water rushed up to meet them. They splashed into frigid water.

Efraim's breath shuddered in his chest. Gaining a foothold in the creek, he pushed ahead. Callie slogged alongside him. Cold water splashed over their knees and soaked their clothes.

Shouts rose from behind them. An engine roared to life.

They pushed faster. A large culvert yawned ahead. He pulled Callie toward it. They had to make this fast. If the men chasing them reached the other side before they did, they'd be trapped inside.

Water rose past their knees. They reached the mouth of the culvert. Efraim released Callie's hand and she stepped into the tube. Pressing his hands against either side of the expanse, he hefted himself up after her.

Crouching, he made for the dim light on the other side of the highway. Current swirled around their legs, moving faster, more powerfully than it had outside. The metal was slick. He braced himself with his hands, waddled as fast as he could on the rounded floor. His feet hit something slippery. He went down.

Callie leaned back for him, gripping his shirt, pulling him up.

The tube rumbled, a vehicle driving on the highway overhead. Shouts from outside faded, their scrambling footsteps drowning the sound, each clunk reverberating as if they were inside an echo chamber. As they inched toward the dim light on the other end, sounds all around them gave way to the roar of rushing water.

They reached the tube's mouth.

Water rushed past them and swirled around their legs. He looked over the edge. A fifteen-foot drop-off gaped in front of them. The roar of cascading water blotted out all sound, even the thrum of Efraim's heart.

Back. They had to go back.

He twisted around, looking over his shoulder while still holding on to the ridged walls for balance. At first he couldn't see the dim light on the other side of the culvert at all. Then his eyes adjusted. The other end was there all right. But it was blocked…blocked by a man, maybe two, sloshing through the water toward them.

He'd led Callie to a dead end. And there was no way out but down.

Chapter Eleven

"How deep is that water?" Efraim asked.

Callie stared down at the black water that seemed so far below. She glanced back at the men fighting their way toward them. Some local she was. They must have changed this when they had rebuilt the highway. She'd been away so long—living in Washington, traveling around the world—that she didn't even know her own town anymore. "I didn't even know there was a drop-off here."

"We're going to have to jump."

She felt his words like a quake in her chest. "Okay." She just prayed the water below was deep enough. If it wasn't, and they hit bottom...

She took one last glance behind them. The clang of their pursuer's progress through the pipe grew louder, closer. Not that they would survive if they stayed here. "Let's go."

"On three. One...two..."

"Hands. Let me see your hands."

The Russian accent made Callie's heart feel as if it would explode from her chest.

"*Three.*"

She and Efraim both stepped off the edge. The night air whistled past her ears. She tried to spread out her body mass, as she'd learned in swimming lessons, scissoring her legs open, spreading her arms out.

They hit the water with a smack. She felt the surface's slap through her feet, her jeans. Her bare arms stung. The frigid water closed over her head just as her feet hit rock.

The force jolted up her legs. She bent her knees, taking the blow. Then pushed herself to the surface.

When her head broke through the water, the current had already pushed her downstream farther and faster than she anticipated. She treaded water and struggled to get her bearings as the water swept her along. The bank rose like a shapeless hulk.

Efraim. Where was Efraim?

She couldn't see him. She could hardly see anything. A clump of trees there. And there...

Headlights glowed from the highway over the culvert. The silhouette of a man stood in front of the glare.

Water swirled around her and gurgled over the rocks along the shore. Her whole body ached with the cold like an infected tooth.

Efraim had to be here. He had to.

Possibilities raced through her mind, each worse than the last. Efraim hitting the rocks at the bottom. Efraim seized by the frigid temperatures, his muscles locking up, current pulling him under. Efraim shot.

She shook her head. She hadn't heard a shot. He had to be here. He had to be alive.

The creek kept moving, pushing her along. The dark outline of the shore moved past. So close, yet seemingly impossible to reach. She scanned one side of the bank, then the other.

Wait.

She saw something dark near the shore. Efraim's hair.

She forced her arms to stroke, her legs to kick. She swam sideways toward the bank, not fighting the current, letting it sweep her downstream. Her jaw shook, her teeth chattering. Her muscles felt stiff and sluggish from the cold, but she pushed on.

She lost sight of Efraim in the dark water. Trying not to panic, she kept moving toward the shore, in the direction she'd last seen him. Her feet hit slippery rock, and she struggled for a foothold, half stumbling, half swimming.

She felt his arms around her before she saw him. He brought her hard against his chest and pulled her up, and into shallow water. Then his lips were on hers. Warm, so warm. When he ended the kiss, he just looked at her, his face inches away. His taut expression collapsed into a look of relief she felt echoed in her chest.

She clung to him for a moment, unable to speak, unable to move up the steep bank, unable to do anything but shiver. He held her tight and rubbed his hands over her arms, her back. Somewhere dogs barked.

"We have to get out of here. Can you stand up?"

Her whole body shook. Her muscles clenched against the cold. It seemed ridiculous. The day had been so hot. But now hours had passed since nightfall, and the sun's heat had long since faded. "I don't know."

"I have to get you warmed up." He rubbed harder.

"The men after us…"

"We were swept around the bend in the creek. It should take them a while to figure out where we are."

"They'll come after us."

"I don't think so. Sebastian's men, my men, they'll be here soon. They might be here now."

"And the sheriff's department."

"Yes."

Another shiver seized her.

"These cold, wet clothes...I have to get you dry." He placed her arms around his neck and struggled to his feet. Water swirled and gurgled around his boots. He splashed the remaining two feet to the shore, cradling her in his arms.

The dogs' barks grew louder and erupted in snarls. A light hit Callie in the face, blinding her.

"Stop right there," said a man's commanding voice. "I have a rifle, and I ain't afraid to use it."

Callie's heart sank. She tried to catch Efraim's eye, but his attention was riveted to the man behind the spotlight. The man pointing a rifle at him.

Please, not again.

EFRAIM SQUINTED into the bright light. He'd been held at gunpoint and blinded with spotlights twice in the past six hours. It was starting to get a little old.

"We're unarmed." Efraim raised his hands to prove the point.

"Sit and hush up," the man ordered the dogs.

The barking stopped.

The relentless glare of the light didn't. "Who are you two?"

"My name is Callie McGuire and this is Efraim Aziz. My family owns the Seven M Ranch."

The man grunted. Either he hadn't heard of Callie's family's ranch or he didn't care for the McGuires. He shone the light on Efraim. "Aziz? What kind of name is that?"

"I'm from a country called Nadar. It's a small island nation in the Mediterranean Sea."

"Arab?"

There it was. Efraim would be lucky if the man didn't shoot him as soon as he heard the answer, but he'd be damned if he was going to lie about his proud heritage. "Yes. I am of Arab descent."

"So what the hell are you doing in my creek? And on this cold night?"

"We didn't realize it was so deep. We were swept a bit downstream," Callie simplified. Her voice shook so badly, it was hard to decipher the words. "We didn't mean to trespass."

"Well, why don't you get out of that water, then? You're going to freeze to death."

Efraim couldn't have stated it better himself. He steadied Callie on her feet and helped her up the bank.

One of the dogs growled.

"Knock it off," the man snapped.

The dog was silent.

Efraim felt Callie shiver. There was no wind, the air had calmed in the hours since sunset and was now as still as death. But there didn't have to be a wind. The temperature had dropped to the fifties. Soaked to the skin, Callie and he could lapse into hypothermia if they didn't warm up soon. "Is there somewhere we can go that is warm? Callie is freezing."

"Of course you're freezing. Damn fool thing to do, swimming in the creek."

Now that they were out of the water and the light wasn't shining in Efraim's eyes, he could see the man's face in the dim night. Lines fanned out from the outer corners of his eyes and creases bracketed his mouth. Sparkles of gray ran through brown hair. He probably wasn't that much older than Efraim. Ten years at the most. And Efraim found it a bit amusing that he was treating them like teenagers caught skinny-dipping on a cold night.

At least he would find it amusing if they weren't freezing to death on the spot. "We need to get warm." He thought of his cell phone, Callie's BlackBerry, useless after their dip in the creek. "And we need a phone."

He expected the guy to raise his gun again and threaten to call the police. Instead, he gave a nod and trudged away, motioning for them to follow. The dogs fell in at the man's heels.

Efraim wrapped an arm around Callie's shoulders and pulled her close as they followed behind the man and dogs. She was still shivering, her body moving in jerky spasms. His was, too, but somehow his mind could only focus on her.

They left the taller vegetation along the creek bed and walked through a small field of scrubby grass. The man's light beam revealed a modest ranch ahead. A rickety barn, some barbed wire fence and not much else. A trailer home sat among a scrub of low evergreens. Light glowed through curtained windows.

"It ain't much, but it's home."

"It looks great to me, sir. What a beautiful setting." Callie's voice trembled in time with her chattering teeth, but her voice rang with sincerity.

Efraim looked at the broken-down place, trying to see the beauty that Callie obviously saw.

"It's warm and dry at least." The man led them to the trailer. He mounted the handful of stairs, the steel ringing with each step. Opening a ripped screen door, he motioned them inside.

The inside of the trailer was about as luxurious as the outside. A threadbare plaid couch lined a wall of the tiny living area along with a pleather recliner. The room opened to a kitchen with cheap vinyl floors and a folding table and chairs. The only thing that was worth more than a hundred American dollars in the whole place was the flat-screen television sitting on a laminated wood stand.

"George? What is—" A woman wearing a terry-cloth robe stopped dead in the middle of the living room. She looked to be around the same age as the man, and just as worn. But instead of shot with gray, her hair held a monochromatic reddish-brown luster that had obviously come straight from a bottle. She smoothed her palms over her hair and focused on her husband. "Why didn't you tell me we had guests?"

He gave a shrug.

The dogs bounded into the house, two bundles of wagging tails and lolling tongues. Efraim couldn't begin to guess the breed of either.

"You're soaking wet!" The woman sounded horrified.

"Good reason for that, Mercy. Found them in the creek," the man said.

"Well, let me get you some dry clothing. Come with me, dear." Mercy motioned to Callie. "George? You get some of your clothes for that young man."

George and Callie followed the woman into the bedroom.

Efraim had to laugh. At thirty-eight, he was hardly a young man. And after the last day or so, he felt older than the sea.

One of the dogs ambled over to him and sat on his foot. He shoved his snout under Efraim's palm and scooped his hand onto his black head.

Efraim scratched behind his ears. After the jump into the water, his rib cage had ached as if someone was beating his side with an ax. The cold had given him a bit of numbing relief. But now as he even started to grow marginally warmer, his side had resumed its ache.

The man returned carrying a pair of faded jeans, a flannel shirt, a thick leather belt and tube socks. "Here you go. Afraid you're going to have to go commando."

Efraim took the clothes. "That's fine. Thank you."

"There's a bathroom over there. Clean towels on the shelf. Help yourself. That is, if Bud will let you go. That's his favorite thing, having his ears rubbed." He clapped his hand on his thigh, and the dog reluctantly stood, releasing Efraim's foot.

When Efraim emerged from the airplane-size bathroom, Callie was sitting on one of the folding chairs in the kitchen. A towel wrapped her hair in a blue turban, bringing out the striking marine color of her eyes.

The woman, Mercy, had turned on the oven and

opened the door. Heat emanated through the kitchen in waves. She grabbed another metal chair and plunked it next to Callie's. She took his wet clothing and hung it on another chair next to Callie's wet jeans and T-shirt. "Coffee will be ready in a jif."

He could already smell the dark, rich scent. Seconds later Mercy took their cream-and-sugar orders and placed a big steaming mug in each of their hands.

Efraim breathed deeply...well, as deeply as his ribs would allow. "Thank you."

Mercy waved his words away and bustled back to the sink. "Don't mention it."

Efraim glanced at Callie. "It's the middle of the night. You didn't have to do this."

"Don't be silly."

He wasn't being silly. He was being grateful. He hadn't seen a lot of kindness lately. Not in America. Not even among his own people. The kindness of Mercy and George made him feel as warm as the coffee, the clothing and the stove.

He reached toward his soaked trousers. "Really, I can p—"

Callie shook her head in a warning.

He bit back the rest of his words. Too late.

Mercy turned from the sink and scowled at him. "I sure hope you weren't going to offer to pay. That would be ridiculous, and I won't have that in my home. You're our guests. Isn't that right, George?"

"Yep," her husband called from the living area.

"Thank you. I didn't mean to offend you, though. I just wanted you to know how much we appreciate what you've done."

"No more than you would do for others, I'm sure."

Efraim stared at the glowing coils in the electric oven. He'd like to think that was true. These people had opened their home in the dead of night to strangers, clothed them, warmed them, taken care of them. All without accepting a dime, even though from the look of things, they could use it.

"He wanted to use a phone, too," George mumbled, still in the living room. He squinted and paced the room in circles. "Can't find the damn receiver."

"Here, let me help." Mercy bustled into the adjoining room.

The dog shuffled over to Efraim and resumed his position under his palm.

Callie turned to him with a tired smile. She was no longer shivering, and her cheeks were a delicate shade of pink that made her eyes twinkle even more. "See? I told you Americans aren't all bad."

She was teasing, but he couldn't ignore the stab of recognition. He'd certainly thought badly of Callie's family, the protesters in Dumont and just about every other American who'd snagged his attention. He'd held their fear and prejudice against them. And in his mind, he'd decided they were emblematic of all Americans. He'd told himself only Callie was different. But he'd been wrong.

He'd let his own fears, his own prejudice paint an entire country with the same brush, and he, of all people, should know better.

Mercy didn't know him, didn't know Callie, and yet she opened her home to strangers her husband had fished from the river. She trusted them when she'd had no reason to trust. She'd taken care of them simply because they needed care.

He cradled the hot coffee in his hands and offered Callie a tired smile. "You're right. And when this is all over, I want you to show me more of your country. I want to see it through your eyes."

Chapter Twelve

One call and a few minutes later Kateb and one of Sebastian and Antoine's men were outside the trailer waiting for them in one of the rented SUVs. The two men were heavily armed, and Mercy's forehead furrowed as she studied them. "I hope the two of you will stay safe," she said, handing them their still-damp clothing.

"Let me at least give you money for the clothing."

"Money? Heavens, no. These are old." She pursed her lips together. "But if you like, you can return them when you're done with them."

Callie nodded. "Yes. That's what we'll do."

They climbed into the backseat of the SUV, and Efraim felt a little sense of regret to be leaving these people without any concrete way to show them his thanks. Maybe when they sent back the clothing, they could fill the pockets with cash. He wondered if Mercy would find a way to send that back, too. Probably.

On the drive home, Kateb filled him in on the Russians. The men hadn't left the highway, and were still there when the deputy arrived. They'd driven past them, answering the lawman's questions when they'd entered town. And when the deputy had let the Russians go, they'd returned to the diner.

"At least they won't track us to George and Mercy's place," Callie said. "I'd hate to have something happen to them just because we had the bad luck to wash up on their property."

"I'll have someone keep an eye on them and make sure they're okay." With the repeated attacks on all the members of the coalition, he wasn't sure where he'd find the manpower, but he'd manage. He certainly wasn't going to let harm come to Mercy and George, not after the kindness they'd showed.

Callie stiffened in the seat beside him.

He tried to read her expression, but all he saw was alertness and determination. "What is it?"

"My family. The truck is registered to Russ."

Retaliation against her family. He hadn't thought of that. "We'll send a car for them. I'll arrange some rooms at the resort."

"They'd never go. Knowing my dad and brothers, they'd rather hunker down with their guns and dare the Russians to show up. But I'll try." She reached for her waist. "Oh, shoot."

He could guess the problem. "Your BlackBerry."

"I forgot it's ruined."

His was, too. He reached a hand over the seat. "Kateb? We need a phone before we lose a signal."

Kateb didn't move. "I don't have mine with me."

Interesting. Efraim knew for a fact that Kateb always had his handheld with him. In fact, he thought he remembered seeing it on his belt tonight.

So why had he lied about having it with him? Was

he afraid Efraim would see something on it? Something he was trying to hide?

He thought of the text message. The message had stated that the car bomb was meant to kill all of the royals, not just Amir. It had directed the dirty investigator to move to plan B. Jane Cameron had taken it back to the lab to try to determine where the text had originated.

Stefan had said that question was still unanswered.

Efraim eyed the back of his cousin's head. He'd pegged Kateb as a lovesick and jealous suitor for Tanya. But just as she wasn't a party girl looking to pick up men, maybe the role Kateb played in this mess wasn't as it seemed either.

Efraim shook his head, not liking where his thoughts were leading. He hated thinking ill of his own people, but Stefan had learned the hard way that he could trust no one. And with the strange way Kateb was acting added to the fact that he'd slept with and given gifts to a woman working with the Russian mob, Efraim needed to be a bit suspicious. "Kateb? I know you have your phone. Hand it to me."

"So she can use it?"

"So Callie can use it, yes."

"You trust her?"

"More than I trust you right now. Yes."

"Very well." Kateb handed Efraim the phone, his expression blank. He turned back in his seat and stared out the window.

Efraim paged through the last few days' worth of communications. All of it seemed like business, all of it legitimate except the six calls to the number Tanya had written on the matchbook she'd given to Fahad.

Efraim let out a breath, more relieved than he wanted to admit. Kateb might be a lot of things they had yet to discover, but he hadn't sent the text about the car bomb and plan B. At least not from this device.

Satisfied, he handed it to Callie. While she was warning her father and brothers, he returned his focus to Kateb. "We met a woman tonight who knows you."

"A woman?"

"In Dumont. Her name is Tanya."

It was dark in the SUV, but Efraim thought Kateb's face took on a reddish tint.

"How many times have you seen Tanya?"

"I saw her when I wasn't on duty. I don't see how it should matter."

"It might matter a great deal."

Kateb glanced at the Barajan driver. "May we talk about this further back at the Wind River Ranch?"

Efraim watched Kateb for a long minute. Was he trying to duck the questioning? Or did he really have something to tell Efraim, something he didn't want the security man from Baraja to hear?

Efraim would trust Sebastian and Antoine Cavanaugh with his life and his country. But he couldn't be so sure about their security men. Could he even trust his own? Could any of them?

"We'll talk further in my suite. Report there as soon as we arrive."

Kateb lowered his head in a bow.

CALLIE KNEW she should go home if she wanted to keep her dad, Brent and probably Russ from storming the

Wind River Ranch and Resort in a misguided attempt to rescue her.

Her dad hadn't really sounded that militant. He'd sounded relieved to get her call telling him she was all right. And as she'd guessed, when she'd told him about the suspected Russian mobsters and the fact that they'd identified Russ's truck and suggested he, Brent, Russ and Timmy pack a bag and come to the Wind River Ranch where they would be safe, he'd told her in no uncertain terms he was safer right where he was, and she would be, too. Then to top it all off, he'd told her he loved her and wanted her to come home.

She shook her head and stared into the crackling fire Efraim's people had waiting for him when they returned. As frustrated as she got with her family sometimes, she knew they loved her. They made that clear even when they couldn't help being big jerks.

But the last thing she wanted to do right now was leave Efraim.

It wasn't as if she was hoping for some kind of romantic encounter. Not that her dad and brothers would believe that, of course. But she had never remembered being so exhausted in her entire life. The last time they'd returned to the resort, adrenaline had made her blood feel like it was buzzing. There had been no way she could sleep. But that was hours ago. Now the sun was starting to lighten the eastern sky. Now she didn't have a single ounce of adrenaline left.

She sat in one of the luxurious leather chairs in Efraim's suite. It felt good. Snug. And even though the smell of the creek water was still on her skin and hair, she doubted even the promise of a hot shower could motivate her to move.

She wasn't sure why Efraim had wanted her to be present for his talk with Kateb, but she was glad he trusted her. She just hoped she could stay alert enough to fulfill whatever role he had in mind.

Efraim motioned for Kateb to sit in the chair next to Callie.

Kateb looked down at her, then back at Efraim. "Are you sure you trust her?"

Callie shifted in her chair. If the man asked that question of Efraim one more time, she thought she might scream.

"Yes."

"You might not after you hear what I have to say."

Efraim glanced at Callie.

She didn't know how to respond. She shook her head, hoping Efraim would see that she hadn't a clue what Kateb was talking about. "If you like, I can leave."

"No." Efraim again motioned for Kateb to sit.

He finally lowered himself to the edge of his chair. He shifted, as if the plush furniture was the most uncomfortable thing he'd ever sat on.

Efraim peered down at him, his expression deadly serious. If not for the ridiculous baggy jeans and flannel shirt, he would look like the picture of a perfect king. In control. In command. His dark eyes able to lay the truth bare in front of him. "Explain yourself, Kateb. Tell me about your relationship with the woman who calls herself Tanya Driscoll."

"My relationship? There is no relationship."

"That is not what Tanya says."

"What did she say? That I was in love with her?"

"She said you gave her a gift."

Kateb smiled, possibly the most cunning smile Callie had ever seen. "Not a gift. A microphone."

Callie sat forward in her chair. "The pendant?"

Kateb didn't acknowledge her, but kept his eyes on Efraim. "I had questions about Tanya. Security questions. So I gave her a necklace with a listening device embedded. I recorded her conversations."

Efraim nodded, as if he was taking it all in stride, unlike Callie who felt like she was about to fall out of her chair. "Who knew you were doing this?"

"No one. I wasn't sure who to trust."

Efraim's dark brows arched upward. "Not Fahad?"

Kateb looked down, as if reluctant to meet Efraim's eyes. "Not at first. I told him yesterday morning. Before I drove you and your horse to the badlands. He had me transfer the recordings to his computer."

"And he wasn't happy."

"No. He thought I should have cleared it with him first."

"Fahad was right." Efraim's voice was firm but unemotional. "He was head of security. Coordinating security efforts was his job."

Kateb shook his head. He was clearly angry with Fahad and frustrated. He reminded Callie of the way her younger brothers often rebelled under Brent's iron rule. Younger brothers resenting older brothers.

"So why didn't you tell him until then? And why didn't you tell me at all?"

Kateb raised his eyes and for the first time, his face held an expression that wasn't about anger, frustration, contempt or cunning. He actually looked as if he was a little ashamed. "I didn't know if I would get anything of value. I didn't want to bother you if all I recorded were diner orders and pillow talk."

"Why did you decide Tanya was worth recording in the first place?" Callie asked.

He refused to look at her just as he had all the other times she'd tried to speak to him. Instead he directed his answer to Efraim. "At the bar the night we arrived, I heard her speaking Russian."

"And you thought she might be working with the Russian mob?" Callie asked. That was the leap she and Efraim had made in the diner tonight.

"Not until the sniper tried to kill Prince Stefan. I didn't think she was a danger until then. That's when I gave her the necklace."

Efraim paced across the floor. He moved with such pent-up power, Callie couldn't take her eyes off him. She had no idea where he was drawing this energy from after the past twenty-four hours, but wherever he got his reserves, they were much deeper than hers.

He stopped at the fireplace and narrowed his eyes on Kateb. "Have you listened to any of these recordings?"

"Some of them. The early ones."

"What did you learn?"

"Nothing that I believed was important at the time." He turned at looked at Callie for the first time. No, not merely a look. A glare.

Shivers scampered down her spine. She raised her chin and met his gaze straight on.

He returned his focus to Efraim. "If I had recognized

something, I would have brought the recordings to you immediately."

"I wish you had. But we will listen to them now."

Kateb shook his head. "When I told Fahad about the recordings, he made me turn them and the receiver over to him."

"So Fahad had them?" Callie asked.

Kateb didn't bring his gaze back to her, and she had to admit after his last glare, she was relieved. He spoke to Efraim. "The American sheriff and that woman, the police scientist who is with Prince Stefan—when they searched Fahad's room, they took his computer."

Efraim gave a low grunt. He strode across the sitting room and disappeared into the bedroom. When he emerged, he held a flash drive in his hand. "I have Fahad's computer files."

Callie smiled. She had almost forgotten their foray into Fahad's room while Jake Wolf and Jane Cameron were waiting for their warrant. Maybe her feelings of guilt had just pushed it from her mind.

Kateb narrowed his eyes on the tiny flash drive. "You copied them?"

Efraim slid into the desk chair. He flipped open a laptop identical to the one Fahad had and turned it on. The computer booted up quickly and soon he had plugged in the drive and was scanning its contents. "Are you sure Fahad downloaded the recordings to his computer?"

Kateb pushed up from his chair and stepped behind Efraim, watching the computer screen over his shoulder. "I'm sure. He also took my laptop."

"He only had one computer in his room," Callie said.

Kateb shook his head. "Mine was there. It had to be."

"In the safe?" Callie guessed. They had assumed Fahad had kept his extra firearms in the safe, but it was big enough to hold a laptop.

Efraim said nothing. His fingers were lightning fast on the keys, and Callie remembered that although he had experience in the military years ago, cybersecurity and encryption was where his true expertise lay. It was why his father had turned over control of Nadar to him, even though the elder Aziz was still young and healthy enough to be more than the ceremonial figurehead he was.

Efraim was to usher his country into the modern age. And part of the pact among the island nations would help develop the infrastructure for such an endeavor, financed by profits from the oil leases off their shores.

Callie leaned back in her chair, letting the softness envelop her, the leather scent wrap around her. The tap of computer keys calmed her, as effective as a lullaby. If she was going to drive all the way back to the Seven M before dawn, she'd better get moving. Otherwise she was going to pass out here in the chair. Better than on the road.

The pickup.

She almost groaned. Russ's pickup was still in the diner's parking lot. And without it, she had no way to get back to the ranch. Not without calling her family or asking Efraim to give her a ride.

"It's not here."

She sat up, her fatigue slipping away as adrenaline she didn't know she still had spilled into her bloodstream. "It has to be."

"No, it's not." Efraim turned to look at Kateb. "There are no audio files in any of the material I downloaded."

The man's shoulders slumped. His arms hung useless by his sides. "Then he erased it."

Callie shook her head. She wasn't following. Not at all. "Erased it? Fahad? Why would he do that?"

Efraim stared at Kateb, waiting for his answer to Callie's question.

"Because he was seeing Tanya, too. I can only assume he was on the recording. And that he wasn't proud of what he was doing."

Callie still didn't see it. "We found the matchbook lying on his desk. If he was so ashamed of his fling with Tanya that he erased all the surveillance recordings, why would he keep her number lying around?"

"That's a good question," Efraim said, still watching Kateb.

"You don't believe me."

"I'm still figuring that out."

Kateb closed his eyes. "I gave the recordings to Fahad. If they aren't there and my laptop isn't there, then I can only conclude that Fahad was trying to cover his embarrassment. Pillow talk. Just as I feared."

Efraim shook his head and raked a hand through his hair. "I can't accept that. Not at face value."

"You don't trust me."

Efraim said nothing, letting the intensity in his dark eyes speak for him.

"You don't trust me. Your blood. Your countryman. And yet you trust her?" He shot a look at Callie that spoke pure hatred.

She tried not to fold back into the chair to get away from it.

"Callie has earned my trust."

"Really?" Kateb's voice cut with a hard edge. "And did she tell you that she and I have something in common?"

Efraim narrowed his eyes on his cousin.

"Yes." That smile again, cunning, mean, as if he was just about to twist the knife and was imagining how good the act would feel. "We have more in common than you know."

Callie had no idea why this man hated her so much, just as she had no clue where Fahad's curses had come from. But whatever it was, she wanted to know. At least then she could face it head-on. She set her chin. "What are you talking about?"

"I told you I heard some of the recordings. The early ones. Conversations. Trysts that Tanya had with other men." His voice was bitter, angry, but the emotion wasn't pointed at Tanya. It wasn't coming from jealousy. His hatred was focused precisely on Callie.

She crossed her arms across her chest but forced herself to hold his gaze.

"What are you trying to say, Kateb?" Efraim did not look pleased with his man, but somehow that didn't make Callie feel much better. She waited for Kateb to go on, her stomach so tight that it ached.

"What am I trying to say? That Tanya didn't only take my brother into her bed, she also took *her* brother." He glared at Callie. "Why don't you ask *her* what happened to those files, that computer. Why don't you consider that *she* might be trying to protect her brother. Or even herself?"

Chapter Thirteen

"Is it true?" Efraim sat in the chair next to Callie's and looked straight into her eyes. He had ushered Kateb out of the suite and ordered him to stay in his room. He didn't know if he should believe the man or not. But he did know he wanted to believe Callie. And whatever she had to say, he needed to hear it.

"I just found out tonight."

He frowned. On some level, he'd been hoping Kateb had made the whole accusation up out of the air. It was disgraceful, hoping for deceit from his cousin, his blood, all to let him continue to believe in a woman who wasn't even from Nadar. Yet at that moment, he would give almost anything for Callie to explain everything away. To fall in his arms. To kiss him. To make love in front of the fire.

He still didn't think that Fahad was right about Callie trying to deceive him. But he was beginning to believe Darek was dead-on when he feared Efraim might want to deceive himself. "*What* did you find out tonight?"

"My brother Russ. He was involved with Tanya, too."

So it was true, then. At least that much of it. "Involved, how?"

"He met her at the Tumbledown Tavern about two weeks ago. He's seen her several times since then."

"Did he know she was working with Russian organized crime?"

"No. I mean, I don't know. I just found out he knew her tonight. I haven't gotten the chance to ask him."

"When did you learn this?"

She licked her lips, obviously uncomfortable. She lowered her gaze.

A weight descended on Efraim's chest. "You chose not to tell me."

She raised her gaze once more, meeting his eyes. "Brent told me at the Tumbledown. I asked if he knew Tanya, and he said Russ had dated her."

Efraim looked away. One more minute of gazing into her eyes and he would be willing to believe anything she said. And forgive anything she'd kept from him. He focused on the stone fireplace. "Your brother Brent. He's the former soldier, right? He is with the protesters?"

"Yes."

A cold image formed in his mind. "He is good with a rifle."

"He didn't shoot Fahad."

"He hates my people. He knows the land. He has the weapons and the skill to use them."

"But he didn't do it."

"How are you so sure?"

She looked down at her hands, twined in her lap. "He said if he wanted you dead, you would be. And he's right. He was an expert marksman. If he was the one who fired that second shot, he never would have missed. But that's not all. As much as he talks, I just can't see him ever committing violence like that. He saw too much of that in Afghanistan. I think that really changed him, coming face-to-face with the horrors that fear and violence can cause. I think that's part of his problem now. He's changed. He wants to prevent violence more than perpetrate it. Not that he'd admit it. Along with the seizures and nightmares, he's afraid that makes him weak."

Efraim nodded. He had to admit it made a strange sort of sense. It was easy to lust for blood if you'd never really seen blood spilled. That was one difference between his brother and him. He'd served in the military. He'd seen the pain violence caused. His brother Faraj hadn't, and he thirsted for the satisfaction he believed violence would bring. He thought strength was about hurting others. He didn't understand that people committed violence out of weakness and fear, not strength. "Your brother Russ? Working with the Russian mob?"

She shook her head. "No, I can't see it. My family, they would hate Russians every bit as much as..."

"They hate me?"

"Yes. That's why I didn't tell you, I guess." She shook her head. "I'm sorry. I should have. I just didn't want you to jump to conclusions."

"You wanted to defend your brother."

"I wanted you to see him for who he really is. Just like I want him to see you."

He let out a heavy breath. Hadn't he recognized her family in himself while sitting in Mercy and George's kitchen? Maybe she was right. Maybe they were more alike than different. All bound by their fears. Could it be that simple? He wished he knew. "Your father?"

"Did he shoot Fahad? No. Never. Dad's a softy, although don't tell him I said that. He isn't even that good with a rifle."

"Your other brother?"

"Joe?" A smile curved the corners of her lips. "Joe is a schoolteacher. He would never go along with some xenophobic protesters' agenda."

"So he's like you?"

Her smile widened. It was one of the most beautiful sights he'd ever seen. "I suppose. He and my youngest brother are the most like me. The most like my mom."

He watched her for a moment without speaking. She held his gaze, her chin lifted and firm. But her eyes looked at him with softness, not challenge. She recognized her family's faults, but she defended them all the same. With all their differences, they were close.

Much closer than he and his family.

Suddenly he wanted to know all about her, how she grew up, what it was like to have a family who was close, what her life on the ranch was like. Everything. But most of all, he wanted to know about *her*. And he had an idea where to start. "Your mother. What was she like?"

"Expansive. Accepting. She loved the ranching life and America but was accepting of other points of view and eager to learn about the rest of the world." She raised her eyes. The blue shimmered with tears that didn't roll down her cheeks. She offered a shaky smile. "My dad always said her love was proof that he had a good heart."

Efraim nodded. As much as he wanted to hate these people, turn the blame of Fahad's death on them, latch on to the same easy answers that Kateb had grabbed, he couldn't. Not when he saw them through Callie's eyes. "Your mother must have been extraordinary."

"She was." She blinked and tears spiked her lashes. "I'm sorry I didn't tell you right away. About Russ, I mean. And there's something else."

He wasn't sure if he wanted to hear more, but he forced himself to ask. Best to get everything out in the open. Then he knew what he was looking at. Then he could find a way to move forward. "What else?"

"Fahad, before he died…" Her voice faltered and faded. She took a deep breath and gripped the arms of the leather chair. "He accused me of manipulating you, of using you."

Efraim would like to feel surprised, but he wasn't. After all Fahad had said to Darek, he knew how his cousin felt. And even more strongly, he knew Callie didn't deserve it. "Forget his words, Callie. I'm sorry he said them, and I know they are not true."

She looked up at him with those big eyes and spiked lashes, as if she wasn't sure she fully believed what he'd said.

It was important to him that she believe. "I trust you, Callie. I want you to feel you can trust me. Next time I want you to know you can tell me anything, and I will accept it."

She smiled and the whole world seemed to be a brighter place. "I have a bad habit of trying to smooth things over before a rift even has a chance to begin."

"You're good at your job."

She shook her head. Her smile fluttered but held, only this time she looked a little sad. "This has stopped being about my job." Again she looked down at her hands.

He stepped closer to her chair. Taking her hand, he pulled her up to him. "What do you mean, stopped being about your job?"

She shook her head, still not meeting his eyes even though her body was only inches from his. "I just want so many things. For my family. For my country. For my world. And for myself."

He brought his hand to her jaw. Her skin was smooth as silk. He could spend eternity touching it and still not get enough. He tilted her face up and peered into her eyes.

Blue as the sea surrounding Nadar. Blue as the field of stars on the American flag. "Wanting many things is not a reason to feel ashamed."

"It is when those things are not possible. It's silly then to hope and want what can never come true."

"What is it that you want?" As soon as the words left his lips, he knew that whatever it was, he wanted to give it to her.

She glanced away from him, suddenly unsure. "Right now, a hot shower."

He thought about the two of them twined together, water and soap bubbles sluicing down their bodies. He would give her that. And more. But there was something he had to know first. Something he had to hear from her lips. "Your family. Do you trust them?"

She didn't hesitate. "With everything."

"Then I will trust them, too." He cupped his hand around the back of her neck and tilted her face up to meet him. He lowered his mouth to hers, lips taking, claiming.

The sweetness of her kiss once again pulled at him, and this time, he let it take him. He was no virgin. At thirty-eight and a prince, he'd experienced his share of women. But with Callie, it was different. Each caress of her lips brought him deeper. Each stroke of her tongue made him need more. He wanted to devour her, to make her part of himself. He simply couldn't get enough.

He skimmed his hands down her body. His fingers trembled, as if he was a boy, as if this was his first time. He grasped the hem of her T-shirt and whisked the cotton up her sides.

She released him, parting only for a moment to help him shuck the shirt over her head and arms. She wore no bra under Mercy's T-shirt, and he drank in the sight of her. Then her lips were back, tempting him, teasing him, making need shiver down his spine and heat pool in his groin.

He moved his hands down over her shoulders, over her back. He settled his hands on her waist and pulled her tight, fitting her to him.

He needed her to be naked. He needed to feel all of her, to be inside her.

As if sensing his thoughts, she moved her hands between them. Her fingers worked quickly on the buttons of the boxy flannel shirt. Soon the stiff fabric parted and the soft warmth of her breasts pressed against his chest.

He let out a shuddering breath. He littered kisses down the side of her neck and nuzzled against her.

"Do I smell like creek water?"

"You smell delicious."

"I feel like I smell like creek water."

He laughed. They probably both did, but he couldn't care less. To him, she smelled perfect, alluring. Maybe it was because he shared the creek smell, but all he could detect was the smell of her skin. And that scent made him want her all the more. "Then let's get you in that shower."

He led her to the bathroom. They stripped off the rest of their borrowed clothes, the bruises over his ribs inspiring concern from Callie.

Getting her naked was a different story. She didn't inspire concern. She inspired pure, shaking need.

The resort's shower was luxurious, but it hadn't struck him how sexy it was until now. A bench rimmed one side of the spacious stone enclosure. Rainlike drops cascaded from multiple showerheads. And the skylight and window overlooking mountains and stars fading into pink sunrise made it feel as if they were part of nature.

It was nice, he had to admit. But all he really needed was Callie.

They slipped under the spray. Water rained down, darkening Callie's hair to light caramel.

He found the shampoo and poured some into his hands. He smoothed it into Callie's wet hair. The scent of jasmine infused the steam. He massaged her scalp then moved his hands down over her shoulders to her breasts.

She washed his hair, as well. She lathered his body, fingers stoking his need for her.

His body was ready to take her. He'd been ready

since he first tasted her kiss. And now seeing her naked, touching her, reveling in the heat of the water and slick, fragrant soap...it was almost more than he could endure.

She moved her hands down his chest and wrapped her fingers around his length. The stroke of her hands nearly sent him over the edge. Grinding his teeth together, he fitted her back against the stone wall and nudged her thighs apart with his knees.

She leaned back, legs open for him. Lips parted, she watched him through hungry eyes. Soap from her hair ran over her breasts, swirling around each nipple. Water cascaded over her flat belly in sheets, coalescing into a waterfall between her open legs.

Hands still around him, she pulled him toward her in ever-more urgent strokes until his tip was poised, ready to enter. She lowered her eyes, watching her hands tease him until he couldn't take it anymore.

"Look at me." His voice was gruff, almost guttural. "I want to see your eyes when I enter...and I want you to see me."

Her lashes fluttered. Her eyes lifted and he seized her gaze. They were so clear that he felt like he could see into her, the very heart of her, and lay bare all her thoughts, her feelings.

And for the first time in his life, he wanted a woman to see him in the same way. His thoughts. His feelings. His fears. And when he pushed into her, sinking into her warmth, losing himself in her eyes, he knew he'd found what he wanted.

Chapter Fourteen

Callie snuggled in Efraim's arms, her cheek pressed against his rib cage, the steady thunk of his heart loud in her ear. The sun must have been up for hours now. Its rays streamed through the shuttered windows. Its height in the sky suggested midmorning. Birds chattered outside the window.

"It's morning." Efraim's voice rumbled in his chest. He smoothed his hand over her hair.

She smiled. When they'd collapsed into bed, their hair had still been wet from the shower. She could just imagine the kinks her straight hair had taken as it dried. Knowing Efraim, his dark hair was probably lying perfect.

She raised her head and met his eyes.

His hair was close to perfection, just a few added waves. His cheeks and chin were dark with stubble. Where he was always handsome, he now looked rakish. Downright hot. And despite engaging in much lovemaking and little sleep, she felt that warm hunger for him growing inside her.

She didn't want this to end. "If you close your eyes, you can almost pretend it's still night."

"And the birds? How do you explain them?"

"Some birds sing at sunset."

"I like how you think." He pulled her close and kissed her.

She let him take her, soaking in the taste of his lips and the heat of his bare skin. She'd wanted him for a long time, it seemed. The moment she first met him, if she was honest with herself. But never did she imagine she would feel this kind of bond between them in such a short time.

From the first time they'd locked gazes, she'd known he was sexually attracted to her. It was plain in the way he looked at her. The way his eyes lingered on hers. The way he noticed every move she made. She liked that he found her hot. But it just wasn't enough. Not coming from him.

She'd wanted everything.

Now as they kissed, she couldn't stop the kindling hope snapping to life deep in her chest. If Efraim could open himself to her as he had last night, if he could listen to her and trust her when she explained her family to him, maybe he could also accept everything she was.

It was a wild hope, she knew. She'd never found a man with that kind of capacity before. But of all the men she'd ever known, Efraim was the most extraordinary in every way.

Maybe she was setting herself up for a fall, feeling these things after they'd been together such a short time, but she couldn't stop. She didn't want to stop.

The telephone's ring jangled through the room.

Efraim gave her one last deep kiss. He groaned as he

pulled away. "I don't know who this is, but it had better be good."

He pushed himself up to sitting, grabbed the receiver and brought it to his ear. "Yes?"

Callie could hear the buzz of a male voice on the other end of the line, but she couldn't identify the caller or hear what he was saying. She glanced at the clock on the bedstand. Eleven o'clock. The reality of what kind of storm was waiting back at the ranch ran through her like a splash of ice water.

She threw back the covers.

Efraim held out a hand, as if to stop her.

She shook her head. Pantomiming, she crooked her left wrist and pointed, as if she were still wearing the watch ruined in the creek.

Efraim let out a sigh and released her. "This afternoon? Yes," he said into the phone.

She climbed out of bed. She could feel Efraim's gaze on her, skimming her body. Out of the corner of her eye, she could see his body, as well, revived and ready for her. She wanted nothing more than to fold herself into bed beside him. She knew when he hung up the phone, he would accept her back into his arms.

But as much as she wanted their time together to go on forever, she couldn't do it. If she wanted the dream, Efraim as part of her world as well as being part of his, she needed to get back to the ranch. She needed to lay the groundwork with her family. The challenges facing them had only just begun.

"All right. I'll be here." Efraim hung up the phone.

Callie had located her own jeans and T-shirt, now fully dried after their dip in the creek. She wished she had something else to wear. The creek water tinge made this morning's jasmine-scented shower fantasy they'd lived only a few hours ago seem like just that—a fantasy. "Who was that?"

"The sheriff. He wants to question me."

Suddenly feeling self-conscious, she grabbed the clothes and slipped into the bathroom to dress. She left the door partially open, not wanting to shut Efraim out. "Maybe he knows something about Fahad's computer. Or maybe he found Kateb's when he searched the room."

"Do you think he'd tell me if he did?"

"Probably not. But you never know."

"You're going back to your father's ranch?"

Callie knew he meant the question to sound casual, but she picked up the tension behind his words. "I'm sure they guessed that I stayed here with you. I have to talk to them. Make them understand how I feel."

"I don't like the idea of you leaving."

She frowned. After their conversation last night, she hadn't expected this from Efraim. She thought he'd moved beyond suspicion where her family was concerned.

She finished dressing and peeked her head out of the bathroom. "They're my family. I trust them."

"I know. That's not what I'm worried about."

She tilted her head, waiting for him to go on.

"I don't believe in coincidences. Tanya sought out Fahad and Kateb to get to me."

The pieces shuffled into place in Callie's mind. "And you think she sought out Russ for a similar reason?"

"How many people know you work for the Office of Foreign Affairs?"

She didn't have to think hard about that one. "Quite a few. Dumont is pretty proud of the success stories of its citizens."

"So anyone who cared to know?"

She nodded.

"Add that the timing of your trip home coinciding exactly with our trip here…"

"And Tanya chose Russ to get to me." She'd been worried that leaving the truck at the diner would lead the mob back to Russ and the Seven M. But Efraim was right. Tanya hadn't dated Russ by accident. They'd already targeted her family.

"Russ's truck. Can someone give me a ride to pick it up?" She tapped her pocket to make sure the truck keys were still there.

They weren't.

"My keys. They must have fallen out of my pocket."

"Not exactly." Efraim pushed out of bed and crossed the room naked. He looked just as wonderful as he had in the shower last night. Powerful and lithe. Maybe even better because in the brighter light she could see every detail of his body.

Except the bruise on his side. It looked horrible, red settling into a dark purple.

She reached for his side. "Does that feel as bad as it looks?"

He stopped next to her, close enough to touch. "I was hoping you were looking at something other than my bruises." One side of his lips crooked up in a smile.

She couldn't help it. At the suggestion, her eyes moved over the rest of him, taking in all the other details. Warmth shimmered low in her belly. She tried to ignore the feeling. And the fact that he was standing so close, she could take him in her hand right now. "I really have to go."

"You're sure?" He took a step closer.

She couldn't fight back a smile. "Yes, I'm sure. But later..."

"I'll hold you to that." He moved past her, opened the hall door and stuck an arm outside. After picking up something from the hall outside, he closed the door and held up a set of keys on a Wyoming key chain dangling from his fingers. "I had some of my men pick up the truck. It's in the front parking area."

"Thank you." He really was amazing. She gave him a kiss, folding against warm skin and firm muscle. When she ended the kiss, her whole body was flushed. "I... um...I have to go."

He gave her a smile. The expression faded as quickly as it came and a frown of concern took its place. "You'll be careful?"

"Yes."

"And you'll come back?" He slipped his arms around her.

"I smell like creek again. The clothes."

He lowered his mouth to hers and kissed her again, deeper. Then he drew in a long sniff. "You smell delicious to me."

"Liar."

"If the creek smell bothers you so much, we can take another shower. But I have to tell you, if it was my choice, we'd skip the shower this time and go back to bed."

She smiled. "This smell really doesn't bother you?"

"Nothing about you bothers me. Not one thing. I'll take it all."

Warmth flooded her. She kissed him one more time. She might not be able to stay, but he'd given her what she needed anyway. And with each kiss, she felt as if she could face a world of challenges and make each one turn out all right.

EFRAIM HATED that Callie had to leave, but he understood. It wasn't just about warning her family; she also had to sort things out with them. Things about him. So when she promised to come back as soon as she could, he reluctantly let her go, took a quick shower to smooth his hair, shaved and wolfed down a room-service breakfast. He had plenty of time left before Sheriff Wolf arrived.

Despite staying in bed until nearly afternoon, they hadn't gotten a lot of sleep. Still, compared to the fatigue of the night before, he felt sharp and refreshed and ready to take on all he must.

He suspected he had Callie to thank for that.

After dressing, he booted up his laptop and started going through the files. He wished he had Fahad's computer instead of leaving it to the sheriff. If the recordings had been downloaded to the machine, they would leave a trail, even if they were erased. Nothing could ever be completely deleted from a computer. And even if he couldn't fully recover the recordings, he'd know if Kateb was telling the truth.

There had to be something he missed.

Last night he hadn't been able to get into Fahad's secure files. Efraim knew what was in them. Security specifications. Passwords. Many of them Efraim's own information that Fahad might need to access in a pinch. If he'd had time in Fahad's room, he could have found the combination to his hotel safe among the encrypted files. He was sure the sheriff had emptied the safe, but with a little more time and a dose of luck, he might be able to find out what Fahad did with the audio surveillance recordings of Tanya. He doubted they had disappeared into thin air.

Especially if Fahad thought he could use them to convince Efraim of Callie's duplicity.

But he would hide them. Keep them secret until the moment he thought he could sway Efraim. Then he would present much the same argument Kateb had last night. Only Fahad would then trot out the goods to back it up. The recordings had to be here somewhere.

Or perhaps not.

And idea shot through Efraim's mind. That was it. Why hadn't he seen it before?

His fingers flew across the keys. It was so clear to him now. So simple. He couldn't find the recordings in the material he downloaded from Fahad's computer because the audio files weren't there. Fahad had parked them somewhere on the internet. A place where he could retrieve them when he needed. And a place Kateb didn't know about.

Fahad wanted to discredit Callie, but he also wanted

the credit for recording Tanya. Kateb was right. Before Fahad went to Efraim, he intended to edit the recordings to cover his own transgressions. But he also wanted at least some of the credit for eavesdropping on the Russian mob.

Sibling rivalry at work.

Efraim's mind raced as fast as his fingers. He scanned the files of passwords, looking for anything that might pertain to a file-sharing site or some other place where Fahad could upload audio files, park them and then download them again without being traced.

There it was.

It was a file-sharing website called Cloud Nine. A collection of music files and short video clips and everything else under the sun. Fahad would only have a password to a site like this for one reason. The recordings of Tanya had to be there.

A few seconds and Efraim was on the site. Finding Fahad's password had been easy. Finding what he'd uploaded to a site packed full of files from all over the world was a lot more challenging.

At least he had an idea of when his cousin had parked the file. Narrowing the search to the hours before he'd left for the badlands the previous morning, he sorted through file after file.

Late morning moved into afternoon, and still he hadn't found anything. He kept slogging, watching the clock out of the corner of his eye. Any second Sheriff Wolf would be here, and Efraim would have to cut his search short. He tried to scan the files faster. He couldn't stop now.

When he finally found something, he was more confused than elated.

It wasn't an audio file, but a small message written in Arabic. A simple message.

Witness to car explosion. Might be able to locate A.K. Will resolve.

Efraim's blood buzzed. He read the message again and again and came up with the same thing each time.

A.K. Amir Khalid.

It couldn't be a coincidence, could it? Details swirled through his mind. Fahad couldn't have written this message, could he? Perhaps Efraim had gotten that part wrong. Perhaps Fahad had gone to the site to upload the audio and found this message instead. And if that was the case, who had posted it? Efraim couldn't say. But knowing Fahad, he'd guess that his cousin hadn't come out to the badlands merely to protect him. He'd also come to tell him what he'd found.

A witness. Someone who might know how to find Amir.

And whatever else Fahad knew about this witness had died with him.

Chapter Fifteen

Callie arrived at the ranch just as her dad and Brent were getting ready to head out. She eyed her dad's old pickup. Here she'd thought Russ's was dirty. She should be grateful she hadn't had to drive Efraim around in her dad's. More dust-colored than blue, the pickup was so filthy that it could blend into the rock formations in Rattlesnake Badlands. The interior was crammed with gear and a jumble of fast-food wrappers. The truck's bed held bolt after bolt of wire.

"Came home to help us string fence, Callie?" Brent called as he loaded one last bolt of wire.

Callie actually liked stringing fence almost as much as she liked working cattle. It was always a nice break to get her hands dirty with physical work after dealing with the delicate negotiations and the figurative dirt of Washington. It was also reassuring to hear the old teasing lilt to Brent's voice, even though he must know she spent the night with Efraim.

She gave her brother a smile. "I'll have to take a rain check, Brent."

"You sure? Dad thinks just he and I are going to

finish the south pasture and lend Helen a hand with the fence she has running along the badlands."

"Helen is going to accept his help?"

Brent chuckled. "I know. I think Dad is fooling himself. I'm betting we get there and she insists on doing it all herself, same as always."

Callie couldn't help but laugh. Helen was a good woman, and she and Dad seemed to be good for each other. But both were so obstinately self-sufficient at times that she wondered if either would ever risk admitting needing the other in any way.

"How am I fooling myself this time?"

Callie turned to see her dad walking from the direction of the house. He looked tired, as if something was weighing on his mind. Callie had a guess as to what that might be. "Hi, Dad."

"Hi, baby." He strode straight for her and took her in a grizzly bear hug.

She squeezed him back, tears blurring her vision. She hadn't fully realized how worried she'd been that her dad was angry with her about last night. The evidence that he and Brent both seemed to love her, even if they weren't crazy about Efraim, made everything a lot easier.

She looked up at her dad. "About last night, Dad..."

He held up a hand. "You're a big girl, Callie. We forget that sometimes, especially Brent and I. But your personal life is your own. You have to do what makes you happy. And as long as you remain happy, we'll try our damnedest to adjust."

She glanced at Brent, and he gave her a nod.

She wasn't sure where this new attitude had come

from, but she was glad for it. "I appreciate this more than you know."

Her dad smiled. "Your mom would approve, I'm sure. If she were around, she probably would have forced our minds open a little wider before now."

"I really do care about him, Dad. And he cares about me."

"I know, honey."

Brent grunted. "But if he does anything out of line, you let us know. Promise, Callie?"

Callie had to laugh. "Big brother to the last."

"Damn straight."

Callie's dad gave her one last hug, then strode for the truck.

Callie glanced around the yard. "Where's Joe? Can't he help with the fence?"

"Joe's taking Lori for her ultrasound."

In all the trauma of the past days, Callie had forgotten her sister-in-law's schedule. The last time she'd talked to Joe, he'd been out of his mind excited about seeing ultrasound pictures of the baby he and his wife were expecting. He wanted a boy to go with the adorable little girl they already had. "And Russ and Tim?"

Her dad paused, half in the truck, half out. Again, his face seemed creased with worry. "Tim is not feeling good. Russ is working around here today so he can keep an eye on him." He slid fully behind the wheel. He and Brent closed their doors and with a wave, they started down the utility road leading to the south pasture.

Callie let out a breath. That had gone better than she could have possibly imagined. She eyed the house. She needed to go in and check on Timmy, but she didn't want to wake him if he was asleep. She'd check with Russ first.

Of course, she had more reason than that to talk to Russ.

She found him mucking horse stalls in the barn. She stopped outside the stall he was cleaning, and he looked up from his work. Leaning his hands on top of the manure fork, he gave her a dry look. "How generous of you to bring my truck back."

She knew she should have rented her own car. She hadn't because her dad had promised she could use one of theirs. No, not just promised. Insisted. Apparently he hadn't fully checked with Russ.

Or maybe the thought of Efraim sitting in the passenger seat had soured Russ on the idea of lending it. "Actually I was wondering if I could still borrow it."

"Sure. Whatever." He scooped a pile of manure into the wheelbarrow. When she didn't move, he paused and eyed her again. "What?"

"How is Tim doing?"

He looked away. "Fine, I guess."

"Has the sheriff talked to him yet?"

"No. Guess he's too busy."

"Murder will do that."

Russ shook his head.

"You don't think a man's murder is important enough to be investigated by the sheriff?"

He gave a shrug. "If it is murder."

"What about Fahad Bahir's death isn't murder?"

Again he shook his head.

She swore sometimes talking to Russ was like talking to a teenager again, even though he was in his early twenties. Maybe she should change the subject. She'd been so buoyed by the acceptance of her dad and Brent that she'd expected it from Russ. If he needed a little more time, she'd give it to him. Now that Brent was being more reasonable, Russ would eventually follow in his oldest brother's footsteps. He always did.

Besides, she had other things to talk to him about.

She paused, trying to carefully choose her words. "I hear you've been seeing a woman from town."

Russ kept shoveling. "I see lots of women from town, sis."

"This one is named Tanya. Tanya Driscoll."

"So? What of it?"

"Has she said anything to you about the royals staying at the Wind River Ranch and Resort? Asked any questions?"

"I don't know." He stopped his work and shot her a bored look. "*Everyone* is talking about your royals staying at the Wind River Ranch and Resort. Maybe she said something, too. I don't remember."

She wasn't sure how to break this to him. Probably better to just spit it out. "I'm afraid..." She bit her lip. No. There had to be a better way to broach the subject of Tanya's real motives.

"You're afraid of what?"

She took a deep breath and pushed forward. "I'm afraid she's been using you."

Russ stabbed the plastic prongs into a pile. Leaning on the handle once more, he peered at her as if she were speaking another language. "You think Tanya's using me?"

"Yes. I'm sorry."

He shook his head. A chuckle sounded from deep in his throat. "Callie, you're not my mother."

"I'm not trying to be."

"Yes, you are. Knock it off."

"I love you, Russ. I want you to be careful." God, she sounded like her dad and Brent when they'd warned her about Efraim. "And there's more. I think—"

"Callie, stop it. Of course she's using me. And I'm using her. I'm not looking to find my soul mate or get married. I'm not looking for scintillating conversations. I just want to have a good time."

"But that's not what she wants."

"What are you talking about?" He shook his head and held up his hand. "Callie, just go back to your sheik and leave me alone. Really."

"This is serious, Russ."

"Oh, serious like you and the sheik? Talk about someone who needs a warning. I hope you don't think you're his only one, Callie. I hear men like him have whole harems of wives. I'm sure he'll make you feel really special."

Callie sucked in a breath of calm. This was going all wrong. She had to explain the situation to Russ. She had to make him understand. "Tanya isn't using you for a good time. She's using you to get to me."

He scoffed at her and pulled the manure fork free. Turning his back on her, he returned to picking the stall, stabbing the bedding with a little too much force and flinging the waste into the wheelbarrow. "You know everything isn't always about you or Brent or Saint Joey."

Oh, God, now he was turning this into a younger

brother's rant against his older siblings. "Russ, I'm serious. We have reason to believe Tanya is working with the Russian mob."

He stopped shoveling in midscoop. "What?"

"She's Russian mob," Callie repeated. She hated throwing it at him like that. But maybe now he'd finally listen, finally let her explain.

"Is this some kind of joke?"

"No joke. Sheik Efraim and the other royals staying at the Wind River Ranch, they are here for an important meeting. A meeting it's my job to facilitate."

"Yeah, 'facilitate.'" He rolled his eyes. "So that's what you were doing last night with the sheik, eh? Facilitating."

"Enough, Russ." She felt her cheeks starting to heat, but she willed the flush away. She wasn't going to let her kid brother embarrass her. She didn't feel ashamed of her bond with Efraim. She wasn't going to take that crap from him. "I'm not joking. This is an important deal. It's very delicate, and it's supposed to be secret."

"And that's why everyone in the county knows about it. Scratch that. After the explosion and corruption scandal, everyone in the *country* has probably heard about it by now."

She sure hoped not, but she couldn't deny that things had gone just about as wrong as they possibly could. "They don't know what the coalition is about. They don't understand what a beneficial deal this could be for everyone involved."

Again with the eye roll.

Sometimes she swore Russ was the baby of the family and not Timmy. God knew, her youngest brother was always thinking of others. Even when he was the one who was hurt, he was trying to take care of her. He was a caring kid. It was Russ who acted like a teenager, from his hormone-based lust for anything with breasts to his immature attitude and temper.

She took another deep breath. By the end of this conversation, she'd probably be hyperventilating just from her efforts to hold on to her cool. "On the other hand, there's also opposition. Someone or many someones are doing everything they can to prevent the Coalition of Island Nations from agreeing to a compact. We believe one of those parties is the Russian mob."

"And that's Tanya." He shook his head. "She's a waitress, Callie. She likes to hang out and hear bands. She's not some kind of spy."

"Open your eyes, Russ. She arrived in Dumont right about the time I was brought into this deal. She happens to latch on to you as well as two different men who work security for Efraim. And last night, we heard her speaking Russian to someone in the kitchen and then two men were waiting for us in the parking lot when we left. They chased us, Russ. We're lucky we got away."

He stared at the dirty pine shavings on the stall's floor, a muscle working along his jaw.

Callie waited a long time for him to speak, the minutes ticking by like hours, marked only by the buzz of flies, the whistle of the wind outside and the deep tones of Dale Watson emanating from the barn radio. Finally she couldn't take it anymore. She didn't know if he was struggling to process all she'd told him or just clamming up, but her patience was gone. "What are you thinking?"

"That she couldn't be a Russian."

"After all you just heard?"

"Being able to speak Russian doesn't mean anything. You speak Russian."

It was true. So did Efraim. "I speak a lot of languages. Russian is only one. And I'm not actually fluent."

"So maybe that's the case with her, too. Only she's better at it than you are."

"You're not facing the facts, Russ."

His shoulders slumped. For a guy who was reluctant to ever admit he was wrong, it was as good as a white flag.

Callie felt bad for her brother. "You couldn't have known."

"So what do I do now?"

"Stay away from her. Don't trust her."

"You told Dad all this?"

She'd spoken to their father last night after George and Mercy had fished them from the creek. "I warned him to watch out for people coming to the ranch. But I didn't put the rest together until morning." Actually Efraim had figured out that Tanya must have been trying to get to her through Russ. But she didn't think pointing out who the realization had come from would help Russ accept it.

"I was wondering why he insisted we carry guns with us while we were doing chores this morning."

"That's Dad."

"Yeah." He threw the fork in the wheelbarrow and trucked the whole thing to the next stall.

Callie watched her little brother move. He was so strapping and headstrong that it was easy to forget he was only a few years older than Timmy. But where Timmy and she had a bond, Russ always seemed to resent her a little. As if he remembered their mother a bit better than Timmy did and resented Callie for not being her.

Callie pulled in a deep breath of pine shavings and the light ammonia smell of used stalls. When she was a kid, she'd worked side by side with Brent and Joe every day. Sometimes they'd talk, sometimes they'd swap nothing but silence, but they'd built a bond by just sharing the same space and the same workload. It had helped them get through the inevitable frictions that came with such different personalities living under one roof.

She stepped away from the stall aisle and ducked into a small room where they kept horse feed and other gear. There had to be another manure fork in here somewhere. She'd help Russ for a while, just work next to him. Maybe it wouldn't make things better, but it sure couldn't hurt.

Sunlight streamed through the window, lighting dust motes swirling in the air. She stepped toward the shovel rack behind the feed.

And stopped dead.

Leaning against the wall behind the oat bin she could see the barrel of a rifle. A shiver of recognition froze her blood.

Heart thumping so hard that she felt like she'd break a rib, she pushed behind the oat bin and picked it up. The stock was dust-covered, but the brass plaque still gleamed in the rays streaming in through the window.

Wind River County Champion Marksman, Junior Women's Division.

Callie's hands began to shake. She carried the rifle out into the aisle and held it up for Russ to see. "Why is this here?"

Russ shrugged. "Where else would it be?"

If he was acting, he was doing a pretty good job. "I lost it yesterday. Out on the BLM. Whoever shot Fahad Bahir took it from Efraim."

Russ looked up from the manure cart. He studied her, then the rifle, his brows dipped low. "I found it out there. This morning."

"And you hid it behind the oat bins?"

He glanced around. "No, I was feeding the horses. I set it there. Must have forgotten it."

"You fed the horses after you rode out on the BLM?" Callie shook her head. Russ wasn't making any sense, and she was afraid to think too much about why.

He shook his head. "I thought you'd be happy to have it back."

"Did you really find it, Russ?" Callie's insides were now shaking so badly that she could hardly stand. Her knees felt uncertain, as if they could collapse at any moment.

"Yeah. Of course. Where else do you think it came from?" His lips flattened into a bloodless line. "You think...you think it was me who shot that guy, don't you?"

She didn't. Did she? "No, I don't think you're a murderer, Russ. Not on your own. But this isn't adding up. I don't think you're telling me the truth."

He narrowed his eyes on her. A flush worked its way

up his neck and colored his cheeks. "You come in here warning me that Tanya's using me, like I'm some idiot, and now you think she talked me into killing a man or something? You think I'm led around that easily?"

"No." And she didn't. He couldn't. "But I need to know the truth."

He waved his arm as if clearing the air of her words. "I told you. I found it. I thought you might want it, so I brought it back. Is that a crime?"

"Of course not."

"Then why all these questions?"

She narrowed her eyes on him. She didn't know what was going on in her brother's head, but she knew one thing. Russ wasn't telling the truth.

A horrible sinking feeling settled in her stomach. "Whoever shot Fahad committed murder, Russ."

"You think I don't know that?"

"The sheriff, he's investigating."

"So? What does that have to do with me?"

"Whoever did this…whoever shot Fahad…he needs to turn himself in."

"You do think I did it, don't you? Let me guess, I did it because I'm so in love with a girl I just met in a bar? And I'm such an idiot that she talked me into working for the Russian mob?"

The whole thing did sound far-fetched, ridiculous. But if it wasn't true, at least Callie had learned something that was. Her brother knew something he wasn't telling her. And she had a horrible feeling that it had something to do with Fahad's death. "I have to go."

"Running back to your sheik?"

"Tell Timmy I'll be back to check on him, okay? And please think about what I said."

"Callie, you think you know everything, but you don't. You don't know anything at all."

She hoped he was right. But she had the feeling she'd discovered far too much.

Chapter Sixteen

Jake Wolf was about as forthcoming as Efraim had feared. Either the man hadn't found anything of value in his search of Fahad's room, or he wasn't about to tell. Efraim guessed it might be a little of both. "Fahad was my blood. I was responsible for him being out in the badlands. I need to know who killed him. Surely you can understand that, Sheriff."

"I understand." Jake Wolf paced toward the door. "And I'm working on finding those answers for you."

"I don't want you to find them for me. I want to help. I want justice."

Hand on knob, Wolf turned to face him. "Justice is my job, Sheik. It is the job of a district attorney and a defense attorney, a jury and a judge. It does not belong to the individual. I will give you answers when I know more."

Too bad Efraim didn't plan on waiting around for the sheriff to feel like giving him answers. He wanted answers now. He'd answered a slew of questions from the sheriff, now he had some of his own. "Have you searched Rattlesnake Badlands?"

"A team has been out there since early this morning."

"A team? What does that mean?"

"Experts, sir."

"Let me guess, their job is justice."

Wolf gave him an emotionless stare. "I must go."

Efraim held up a hand. He shouldn't have been flip. Not when he had more questions to ask. "One more thing, Sheriff. Please."

Wolf nodded.

"Were there any witnesses to the explosion?"

"None who have come forward, no."

"None who have come forward," Efraim repeated. "But that doesn't mean that there are no witnesses out there."

"No, I suppose it doesn't." The sheriff watched him. His eyes showed nothing, but Efraim could imagine he was trying to figure out why he'd ask such a question and if Efraim knew something he didn't.

Ever since Efraim had seen the message on Cloud Nine, he'd debated about showing it to the sheriff. He still hadn't decided what he should do.

"I really must be going," the sheriff finally said. The sunlight streaming in the windows caught his belt buckle. It looked much like Efraim's dagger buckle, the small dagger now lost, the buckle itself blank and worthless. But instead of housing a weapon, the sheriff's depicted a howling wolf.

Another reminder of how Efraim had hoped Wolf would be a kindred spirit. Another reminder of how that hope had never borne fruit.

At least the sheriff had returned his pistol to him. Its weight around his waist felt reassuring, and he needed all of that feeling he could get right now. And judging from what the sheriff had told him, the FBI seemed to be willing to leave him alone. For now.

He moved to the door and opened it for the lawman. "I will be waiting for those answers, once you find them."

The sheriff stepped out into the hall and was gone, leaving Efraim to stew in his own thoughts. Only a day had passed since Fahad had been shot, but it felt like a week. It felt like a lifetime. When Callie had been with him this morning, she'd soothed his frustrations. Now that he was alone, he felt as if he was jumping out of his skin. He couldn't wait until she returned. He needed to tell her about the witness in the message. He needed her to help him figure out what it meant.

He needed her.

There was a time when that realization would have disturbed him. Now it made him smile. He didn't know if he was quite ready to tell Callie he was falling in love with her. They had known each other such a short time. But he felt certain it was true. He was falling in love with Callie McGuire. And he couldn't wait for her to walk back through his door. He couldn't wait to tell her his thoughts and take her back into his bed. He couldn't wait to show her how much he cared.

When he finally heard her knock on the door and open it, he didn't have a chance to do any of those things.

She looked up at him, her body shaking, her eyes red from tears. She set her truck keys on the bookshelf and stood with her hands hanging useless at her sides, as if she had no idea what to do next.

He folded her in his arms. "What's wrong?"

She pressed her cheek to his chest. For a long while, she didn't answer. She just clung to him as if she'd never get the chance to hold him again.

Finally she drew a shuddering breath and looked up at him. "It's Russ. I think he might be hiding something."

Russ. The second-to-youngest brother. The one dating Tanya. "Something? Like what?"

She shook her head. "We need to call the sheriff, turn everything we know over to him."

The sheriff. Efraim had had enough of the sheriff and the way the man allowed information to flow only one way. "You need to tell *me* what happened, Callie."

Tears swamped her eyes. "My dad. He's out stringing fence. I need to talk to him first."

"Callie."

"Please, Efraim. I can't."

"You can't be honest with me?" A tremble centered in his chest.

"I just have to...I have to find out more."

"I asked you if you trusted your family. You said yes."

"I do trust them."

"But you learned something. Something that alarms you. What did you find out, Callie? Tell me, now."

"It's not like that." She shook her head and pulled away from him. "There has to be a reason. Something we don't know."

Cool air settled around him where her warmth used to be. "Did one of your brothers shoot Fahad?"

"No." Her voice wavered.

His throat went dry. This couldn't be happening. Not

with Callie. And yet he could feel her pulling away. Just
as she'd pulled away physically. She was withdrawing,
circling the wagons and leaving him on the outside of
that circle. "I trusted you. I chose to believe you over
Kateb, my own blood."

"And you can still trust me, Efraim. You have to."

He held on to her words. He wanted to trust her.
"Then I will ask again. Did one of your brothers shoot
Fahad?"

"I don't know." She gulped air and pushed on. "But
whatever happened, it's not like we thought."

"Was it Brent?"

"Fahad said something before he died."

Efraim leaned forward. "Fahad?"

"He wished both my family and yours be destroyed."

He shook his head. She'd told him Fahad had said
ugly things about her. But she'd left out this. "What does
this have to do with anything?"

"I thought he was delirious and didn't know what he
was saying. But it was like he was cursing us."

He still didn't get it. "Why are you telling me this
now?"

"Because it's happening. Don't you see it? If we
don't take this slow, learn what really happened, why it
happened…"

"Why it happened? Fahad is dead. Murdered."

"That's not right. He wouldn't do that. There must
be more we don't know."

His mind latched on to the thing she'd said when she'd
first walked in the door, when he was more focused on
his thoughts of her and worries over her emotional state

than on what she was saying. Before he'd wanted to face it. "Was it Russ? Did your brother Russ kill Fahad?"

Her throat moved, as if she was choking back tears.

He had his answer. "Was he working with the Russian mob?"

"No. And I don't know what happened. Please, Efraim. We need to learn the truth before racing into something. We need to know why."

"I don't have to know why." He grasped the keys from where Callie had laid them on the bookshelf.

"No. Don't. Efraim, please. I don't know that Russ had anything to do with it."

"Your eyes say different."

"Please, don't."

He strode into the hall and closed the door behind him, shutting out her pleas. Time for investigation was over. Time for waiting done. Now was a time for justice. And as painful as it was to turn his back on Callie, he knew what he had to do.

Chapter Seventeen

Callie's knees folded. Gripping one of the leather chairs, she lowered herself to the floor. The suite smeared in front of her, a wash of color. Salty tears rolled down her cheeks and wet her lips.

So Fahad had been right after all. Her family, Efraim's, all of them would be destroyed.

No.

She needed to call the ranch, warn Russ. But if she did, she knew her family would greet Efraim with guns blazing. Brent might be the expert marksman, but that didn't mean Russ and Timmy couldn't hold their own. And they had a regular arsenal of hunting rifles in the house with which to get the job done.

The sheriff. She had to call the sheriff. She felt useless without her BlackBerry.

She glanced around the room for a phone. A small, cheap-looking cell phone lay in a jumble of receipts next to Efraim's laptop computer. She picked it up, praying it wasn't the one he'd carried into the creek.

She turned it on and scanned the display. A text sent message flashed on the screen.

She shook her head. The time readout indicated the

text was sent several days ago. Yet she never remembered Efraim using a stripped-down phone like this one.

She chewed her bottom lip. She knew she shouldn't snoop, but something felt strange about this. Something wasn't right.

She brought up a copy of the text. As she read the words, her stomach tensed into a knot.

As soon as he crested the rise and spotted the timber gate announcing the Seven M Ranch, Efraim felt his stomach hollow out the way it had when he'd been a soldier. When it had been his job to fight.

And, if need be, to kill.

He scanned the sagebrush and sparse grass sloping down to the creek, growing more lush the nearer to water. He took in the white house, the fence of pine rail stacked in interconnecting vees, back and forth like an accordion, and the silver shine of wire stretching for miles across the plain. He wondered how it all looked through the eyes of a young girl growing up with big dreams, the only girl with four brothers and a mother who died.

He focused on the asphalt road.

He'd tried to push Callie from his mind the entire drive from the Wind River Ranch and Resort. He still couldn't believe she'd tried to keep the truth from him. The look on her face when he'd guessed the blame rested with her brother Russ cut into his chest like a physical wound. But he really couldn't blame her. She was looking out for her brother, her blood. The same thing he had to do now.

The only thing a man or a woman could do.

Under other circumstances, if they'd had more time to build a bond together, things might be different. Maybe she could have become his family and he hers. But with Fahad's death at her brother's hand, that die had been cast. And there was no going back.

The dream he'd nurtured of the two of them transcending these forces of nature was just that—a dream.

He turned the truck into the drive. Its frame rattled over the cattle guard and tires popped and crackled over gravel. The house looked still, no life, no movement. He drove past it and headed for the barn.

Callie had said her father was stringing fence. Even with as little ranch experience as Efraim had, he knew that job took more than one. Yet Callie had talked to Russ here at the ranch. He could only hope Russ hadn't ventured out onto the land to help. He didn't want to wait, risk the fire in his blood cooling to where he could no longer do what needed to be done.

He had to bring this to an end. Win justice for Fahad. Set things right.

He pulled the truck up to the barn and switched off the engine. Leaving the keys in the ignition, he climbed out, paused and listened to his surroundings.

There was no barking of a dog this time. The border collie either knew the sound of Russ's truck so well that he didn't pay attention, or he was out with Callie's father in the pasture. A dozen horses milled around the corral adjoining the barn. Callie's palomino mare raised her head and nickered, then lowered it to resume searching for sparse blades of dried grass. A mare with a foal by

her side milled in an adjoining enclosure. The soft twang
of country music wafted from a radio inside the barn.
Somewhere a door rumbled open on old runners.

He moved away from the sound, to the small human-
only entrance on one end of the structure. The knob
turned under his hand, but the door didn't move, the
corner stuck. He gave the door what he hoped was a
quiet shove and it swung open.

The door opened into a utility area filled with equip-
ment one might use on a ranch. Next to it was a tack
room that smelled of leather saddles and horse sweat.
Next, a feed room sweet with hay and oats.

He turned into the barn aisle. The music came from
a radio strung high up on the wall. This part of the
barn smelled strongly of pine shavings and alfalfa hay.
A wheelbarrow stood in the aisle piled high with bales.
No horses inhabited the stalls, and Efraim assumed they
were the ones outside in the corral.

"What are you doing here?"

Efraim peered past swirling dust motes. Callie's
brother Russ stood at the end of the aisle, a push broom
clutched in his hands. Like the rest of Callie's brothers,
he was a good-looking kid. Although he might be the
most classically handsome of them all. Efraim imagined
he thought nothing of Tanya passing her phone number
along. It probably happened to him all the time. Efraim
tried to go further, tried to picture the kid agreeing to go
along with Tanya and her friends' plan, but that image
didn't come.

What would make a kid like this sell out his country?
What would make him sell out his sister? A sister who
would give up everything to protect him in turn?

"I said, why are you here?" Russ's voice wobbled a bit. He jutted out his chin in a gesture so familiar to Efraim by now that it made his chest ache. "Callie already left."

"I didn't come for Callie."

"Then why did you come?"

"I want answers."

"Answers to what?"

"I want to know who killed Fahad Bahir."

"Callie sent you?" He craned his neck, as if trying to see past Efraim, even though there wasn't much beyond him but a wall, the doors to the areas he'd walked through off to the side. "Where is she?"

Efraim kept his focus on Russ. "What did you tell Callie this afternoon?"

"I didn't tell her anything." Russ stopped as if realizing that was too close to a confession. "There's nothing to tell."

"You shot my cousin Fahad. You murdered him."

"What?"

"You murdered him."

"I sure as hell did not." The chin tilted up again. So defiant. So brave. So like his sister. "Now get out of here or I'm going to call the sheriff."

"Go ahead and call him. Then you can confess."

"Are you crazy?"

A sound came from behind him.

Efraim tensed but didn't dare take his eyes off Russ. Instead he searched the doorway to the side of him with his peripheral vision but couldn't make out any movement.

Russ craned his neck again. "Dad?"

For a moment, Efraim braced himself, half expecting Callie's father and brothers to barge in, rifles pointed at his back. He risked a glance.

No one was there.

He swung his focus back to Russ. "You told Callie you shot Fahad."

"I did not. Is that what she said?"

"She said you knew something and she wanted to learn more."

"That's not the same as saying I did it. I didn't. I swear." He glanced down at Efraim's waist.

The gun. He'd brought it to threaten the boy, to get answers. He didn't want to think beyond that. But he could tell by the sheen of fear in Russ's eyes that the kid thought he'd come to use it. To put a bullet in him. To take his revenge.

Hadn't he?

Efraim pushed the question to the back of his mind. "Tell me the truth. Tell me the truth and I'll let the sheriff deal with you."

"That is the truth. I didn't shoot him. I didn't shoot anyone."

Another possibility popped into Efraim's mind. "Did you attack me out on the Bureau of Land Management land?"

He shook his head. "The first time I laid eyes on you was when we were riding up and caught you with Callie. I swear."

Frustration wound like a ball just under Efraim's rib cage, making it as hard to breathe as the cracked rib. He wanted to throttle the kid. Beat him in the head until he admitted killing Fahad. The problem was, Efraim sensed Russ was telling the truth. That he hadn't shot Fahad after all. And if that was the case, Efraim didn't know where to turn next. "So you didn't kill Fahad. I believe you. But I also believe you know who did."

Russ's eyes flared wide.

That was it. Russ was protecting someone. That must have been why Callie wanted to ask more questions, talk to her father, find out more. Russ didn't do it, but he knew who the murderer was. "Tell me who did it."

The kid's Adam's apple bobbed, but he didn't speak.

"Was it your father?"

The kid didn't answer.

"Are you going to tell me, or should I just go find him?"

"No...no, it wasn't Dad."

"Then who?"

Russ shook his head. "Don't make me tell you." Tears trickled down the kid's face. He might be in his early twenties, but right now he looked fifteen and scared out of his mind.

Efraim gritted his teeth.

"Please. He didn't have a choice."

"Didn't have a choice?" Efraim focused on those words. Anger coalesced around them, made him feel focused, solid in his purpose again. "Did Fahad have a choice when the bullet plowed into his chest? When it stole his breath? When he drowned in his own blood?"

Russ shook his head. Tears streamed faster, glistening on his cheeks, dripping from his chin.

"Whoever shot Fahad murdered him in cold blood. He deserves to pay."

"No, it wasn't like that. He didn't have a choice."

"Tell me who," Efraim demanded.

"Please, no."

Seeing Russ fade back, hearing the plea in his voice, made Efraim sick to his stomach. But he couldn't walk away. He had to know the truth. "Tell me," he repeated.

"I can't. I won't." The kid's voice hitched with a sob. "But he didn't mean to. He just couldn't let her die."

"Couldn't let her die?" Efraim repeated.

He almost didn't hear the voice come from behind him, low as a whisper. "I did it. It was me."

Chapter Eighteen

Callie jumped out of the car before Sebastian had come to a complete stop. She hit the gravel running. When they'd first turned into the drive, she'd noted the absence of a sheriff's department SUV. Russ's truck sat in front of the barn, a good indication that Efraim was inside. She just prayed Russ wasn't in there with him. Or if he was, that Efraim had paused to ask questions before acting on whatever it was he thought he knew.

Things had gotten so much clearer since he'd left her.

She gripped the cell phone in one fist. She had to show Efraim the text. She'd read it to Sebastian, Antoine, Stefan and Jane, who'd all been in the Wind River Ranch's great hall. All of them had recognized it as the same text they'd found on Jane's colleague's phone. And all had been as shocked as she was to learn the sender was Fahad.

Sebastian had jumped at the chance to help, racing through the winding roads as fast and sure as any native. Callie had been relieved to have him drive. She was so afraid for her family, so afraid for Efraim, she couldn't see straight, let alone navigate the curves. Jane had promised to call the sheriff and she'd left Stefan and Antoine discussing what to do about the fact that Fahad seemed to be at the very heart of the plot against them.

But to Callie, none of it mattered as much as stopping what she feared was about to take place. The problem was, she had no idea how she was going to do it.

She pushed through the door. Voices hit her as soon as she stepped inside.

"Tell me who." Efraim's voice.

"Please, no." Russ.

Callie's stomach lurched. Oh, God. She had to stop this. She had to…

"Tell me," Efraim repeated.

"I can't. I won't." Russell sobbed, the tough twenty-something ladies' man gone. Just a kid left in his place. "But he didn't mean to. He just couldn't let her die."

Then another voice, not much louder than a whisper. "I did it. It was me."

Callie reached the aisle. Her knees faltered. She reached for the door frame and sagged against it. Somehow she'd known it was him. Somehow she'd suspected it. His trip out on the BLM that day. His story about the ATV. The injuries to his face and the way he'd sequestered himself in his room. She just hadn't wanted to face the truth. She couldn't make sense of it. She still couldn't.

Timmy had shot Fahad.

EFRAIM TURNED and faced a boy he'd never met. But even though he hadn't been introduced, he knew who the skinny teenager must be. His hand holding the tiny dagger from Efraim's belt buckle, he stood feet spread, chin up, as if ready to fight to the death to defend his older brother. A brother who had been hiding the truth to defend him.

Callie's youngest brother. Tim. The one she said was so much like her.

Efraim's mind swirled with questions, but only one rose to his lips. "Why?"

"He was going to shoot my sister."

Efraim shook his head. He must have misunderstood. "Fahad? Shoot Callie?"

"He was down on one knee. He had her in his sights. I couldn't let him pull the trigger."

Darek's words jangled in his memory. Fahad had told Darek Callie was a threat. Did he think she was so dangerous to his vision of Nadar that he would try to shoot her? Murder her in cold blood?

"I'm sorry." The kid's wobbly voice cut through his thoughts. "I didn't want to kill anyone. I didn't want Callie hurt. I'm so sorry."

Timmy opened his hand and the tiny dagger clattered to the concrete. His shoulders sagged. "I know you want to kill me. But don't kill Russ. Please. He didn't do anything. He wasn't even there."

"Why did you attack me?"

"I...I thought you'd hurt Callie. Just like him. I thought you were tricking her."

That explained why he'd followed Efraim and not Callie and Fahad. Why he'd run when Callie cried out. Why he'd let them get to the creek without attacking again.

"Are you going to shoot me?"

Efraim followed the kid's gaze to the gun at his waist. He'd come to the ranch for justice. That was what he'd told himself. But he knew in his heart he'd really come to get the vengeance he'd promised Fahad.

Vengeance he no longer wanted.

It had been easy to want to strike out at a shooter he didn't know. A murderer he could hate and didn't have to understand. A faceless enemy who was different from himself.

But this boy?

When he'd come to America, he'd focused on the protesters' fear and anger. That had been easy to hate. To give fear and anger of his own in return. But this boy didn't shoot Fahad out of fear and anger and hate. He was simply protecting a sister he loved.

A woman Efraim loved, as well.

Callie had told him they needed to find out more. She had begged him to trust her. She was protecting her brothers. He'd accused her of that at the time. But what he hadn't understood was she was also protecting him.

And what had he done in return? He'd chosen fear and anger and hatred. He'd seen threats where there was just tragedy. And as a result, he'd nearly compounded it.

He pressed his lips into a grim line. "I'm not going to shoot you."

The boy's face crumpled. Tears cascaded down his cheeks. "I'm so sorry," he repeated.

Efraim dropped his gaze to the floor. Witnessing the kid's fear and guilt and now his relief cut like a sharp blade. He'd done so many stupid things in the past day and a half. So many things of which he was ashamed. He only hoped he could fix things. With Callie. With her family. He only hoped he could make up for some of the hurt he'd caused. "I'm sorry, too."

Efraim sensed Russ move past him, slip an arm around his younger brother, offer comfort, usher him through the utility room and out of the barn. He didn't move. Couldn't move. For the first time in his life, he had no idea what to do next.

"Efraim."

Her voice moved over his skin as light as a caress. He swallowed into a parched throat. "Did you hear?"

"Yes." She stepped into the aisle.

He didn't look up. Couldn't look up. "Did you know?"

"That it was Timmy? That he was protecting me?"

He didn't know why it was so important to him, but he needed her answer. "Did you know when you came to my suite?"

"No." Her voice hitched, and he could hear she was crying. "I just knew Russ was hiding something. I had no idea it was Timmy he was protecting. I should have. Looking back, I should have figured it out. I think I probably just didn't want to know."

He looked up and met her eyes.

They were still the color of the sea, still swirled with emotion and hope and optimism. Still saw things he was only beginning to see. "I'm so sorry I didn't listen to you, that I didn't wait."

She nodded. She took a step toward him. Then another. Then she was in his arms, the length of her body pressed against him, her head resting on his chest.

He pulled in a deep breath of her. She still smelled of jasmine. "I love you, Callie." As soon as the words left his lips, he knew they were true. It was impossible. Ridiculous. They'd known each other only a couple of weeks. Had only really spoken about more than policy issues for a little over a day. Yet it felt as if he'd known her for much longer.

He felt as if he understood her heart.

"I love you, too, Efraim."

Her words were muffled against his chest, but they were the most beautiful he'd ever heard.

She looked up at him, her eyes wet, her lips slightly parted.

He brought his mouth down on hers and she opened to him, took him in, honest and true. And when their kiss ended, he could feel tears wet his own cheeks, and he didn't brush them away. "I want to start over with your family, if they'll let me."

Her lips curved upward in a smile. "I'd like that."

"And America. I want you to show me your country. The places, the customs, the people. I want to see it through your eyes. I want to see the world through your eyes."

"And I want to see it through yours."

He smiled. He felt as if he was beaming.

"What about Nadar? I want to see more of your country, too."

"And you will."

"Do you think your people… Will they accept me?"

He hadn't thought about his country's reaction to seeing their prince in love with an American. He'd been more focused on her country's reaction to him. "I don't know. But I have a feeling they'll come around. In time. I'll see to it. They'll come to love you as much as I do."

She hugged him again.

He could hardly believe he'd found this woman. And now that he had, the world seemed to stretch before him with endless promise and possibility. But before he could claim it, there was much to handle. "Go, talk to your brother. He needs you now."

Callie's eyes welled with tears. "Thank you."

And before he let her go, they kissed again, long and deep. And Efraim knew that no matter what happened from here on out, they would figure things out.

Together.

CALLIE WAS STILL coming to terms with all that had happened. Her heart ached for Timmy, for her family, for herself. And although she'd be grateful forever to her youngest brother for saving her life, she was heartbroken that his act had to cost him so dearly.

Jake Wolf had arrived at the ranch about the time Brent and her dad had returned from stringing fence. They had all gone to Dumont, following Jake's sheriff SUV. They had sat at the jail and waited while Tim was booked. And the moment bail was set, they'd taken him home. She wasn't sure what would happen to her brother, but Jake confided that all the evidence he'd found so far suggested Timmy's story was true, and that he would probably do no time.

Efraim had his own family tragedy to come to terms with. Fahad had been closer to him than his own brother. It was a horrible shock for him to learn Fahad was working with the forces responsible for the car bomb that was designed to kill all the royals, and might have succeeded in killing Amir. She'd felt horrible when she'd shown Efraim the text message about the car bomb and plan B. But Efraim had faced the betrayal head-on. He had done a little more digging and now was displaying what he'd found on an internet file-sharing website and explaining how it all fit together to the COIN leaders ringing the long conference table.

Efraim pointed to the projection of his laptop display on the resort boardroom's retractable screen. "This is where Fahad was getting his orders and making his reports. It's a file-sharing website. He would upload his message or receive his orders, like the last one here, the text about the car bomb and plan B that he then relayed to Jane's colleague. Anyone could access the information. But only Fahad and the person giving him orders would know what it meant." He looked down at the COIN leaders sitting in the leather chairs around the long table. Jane Cameron and Callie sat among them.

Jane frowned. "So can we find out who is giving him the orders? The one he's reporting to?"

"I'm afraid not. That's the idea behind these file-sharing sites. As long as the person posting uses some precautions, it's virtually impossible to trace who has posted to it or viewed it."

"So we've hit a dead end," Antoine said.

"Not exactly." Efraim hit a few keys on his computer. Another image came up. The website again, but this time it was the message he'd discovered. "I captured this earlier. It has since been taken down."

Everyone sitting at the table read the message.

Witness to car explosion. Might be able to locate A.K. Will resolve.

Sebastian sat forward in his chair. "A witness?"

"At first I believed Fahad discovered news of the witness from this website, but I was wrong. He uploaded this message. Somehow he learned there was a witness. And he aimed to take care of him or her."

"You mean kill him or her," Antoine said.

Efraim nodded. "I believe so. There is also a chance they will first use the witness to find Amir. Obviously we need to stop both of these things from happening."

"I'll come up with something," Sebastian volunteered. "I'll find this witness. Leave it to me."

Callie gave him a smile. Both of the twin sheiks of Barajas seemed resourceful, but Sebastian particularly struck her as protective. She had only to remember the way he'd rushed her to the ranch. As it happened, she hadn't had to stop Efraim from doing something rash, but she'd needed to be there. To witness what a good heart he had. To help Tim explain what had really happened to his dad and older brothers and Jake Wolf. To help pick up the pieces and begin to heal the wounds.

"I will keep monitoring this bulletin board. Whoever Fahad hoped would see this message might not be aware that he is dead." Efraim's voice hitched a little when speaking his cousin's name.

Callie's stomach clenched. She knew his cousin's betrayal had struck Efraim particularly hard. All along they'd believed he was a victim of the plot to destroy COIN. It was a shock to learn he'd been part of the plot all along—a very important part it seemed—and Efraim was still reeling from it.

She was sure it would take a long time for him to recover from that blow.

At least he had the people gathered here to help him. She glanced at Stefan and Jane, Antoine and Sebastian. Efraim hadn't been particularly close to any of them before this nightmare had begun. Not like he was with Amir. But she could see COIN growing tighter with each day that passed. And now even Darek might be coming around. The opposition to COIN might actually be making it stronger.

At least she could hope.

Stefan cleared his throat and focused on Callie. "I've heard the Russians are gone. Disappeared. Is this true?"

She nodded. "That is what I've heard from the FBI. They have Tanya's description, but she and the men Efraim and I saw at the diner have yet to turn up."

"I think we should keep a look out, as well," Stefan said. "I doubt we've heard the last of them. One thing we've learned through all this is that we need more answers, and the only people we can rely on to get them are ourselves."

The men exchanged glances and nods.

"I suggest we keep our plans confined to the people in this room whenever possible." This time it was Antoine speaking. "And we take a close look at all those in our employ, including the workers at the resort."

Another murmur of agreement and the meeting ended. Each person set off to do his part, leaving Efraim and Callie alone.

Efraim closed the door behind them and took Callie in his arms. "Is everything okay at the ranch?"

"As okay as possible."

"And with you?"

Her throat felt thick. She nodded, uncertain her voice would function.

"Good. Because now that you're here with me, everything is okay with me, too."

"I'm glad."

"I'm more than glad." He smiled. "I'm in love."

She rose on tiptoe, wanting him to kiss her and hold her and make her feel as if things might one day be okay.

He granted her wish, bringing his lips to hers. And as they kissed, such love welled within her, she dared believe it was enough to heal the world.

* * * * *

*Things are heating up in Wyoming
as danger continues to follow the royals
on their quest for peace.
Next month* COWBOYS ROYALE
continues with RANSOM FOR A PRINCE
*by reader favorite Lisa Childs.
Look for it wherever
Harlequin Intrigue books are sold!*

INTRIGUE

COMING NEXT MONTH

Available March 8, 2011

#1263 RANSOM FOR A PRINCE
Cowboys Royale
Lisa Childs

#1264 AK-COWBOY
Sons of Troy Ledger
Joanna Wayne

#1265 THE SECRET OF CYPRIERE BAYOU
Shivers
Jana DeLeon

#1266 PROTECTING PLAIN JANE
The Precinct: SWAT
Julie Miller

#1267 NAVY SEAL SECURITY
Brothers in Arms
Carol Ericson

#1268 CIRCUMSTANTIAL MARRIAGE
Thriller
Kerry Connor

REQUEST YOUR FREE BOOKS!
2 FREE NOVELS PLUS 2 FREE GIFTS!

◆ Harlequin®

INTRIGUE®

BREATHTAKING ROMANTIC SUSPENSE

YES! Please send me 2 FREE Harlequin Intrigue® novels and my 2 FREE gifts (gifts are worth about $10). After receiving them, if I don't wish to receive any more books, I can return the shipping statement marked "cancel." If I don't cancel, I will receive 6 brand-new novels every month and be billed just $4.24 per book in the U.S. or $4.99 per book in Canada. That's a saving of at least 15% off the cover price! It's quite a bargain! Shipping and handling is just 50¢ per book in the U.S. and 75¢ per book in Canada.* I understand that accepting the 2 free books and gifts places me under no obligation to buy anything. I can always return a shipment and cancel at any time. Even if I never buy another book, the two free books and gifts are mine to keep forever.

182/382 HDN FC5H

Name	(PLEASE PRINT)

Address	Apt. #

City	State/Prov.	Zip/Postal Code

Signature (if under 18, a parent or guardian must sign)

Mail to the **Reader Service:**
IN U.S.A.: P.O. Box 1867, Buffalo, NY 14240-1867
IN CANADA: P.O. Box 609, Fort Erie, Ontario L2A 5X3

Not valid for current subscribers to Harlequin Intrigue books.

**Are you a subscriber to Harlequin Intrigue books
and want to receive the larger-print edition?
Call 1-800-873-8635 or visit www.ReaderService.com.**

* Terms and prices subject to change without notice. Prices do not include applicable taxes. Sales tax applicable in N.Y. Canadian residents will be charged applicable taxes. Offer not valid in Quebec. This offer is limited to one order per household. All orders subject to credit approval. Credit or debit balances in a customer's account(s) may be offset by any other outstanding balance owed by or to the customer. Please allow 4 to 6 weeks for delivery. Offer available while quantities last.

Your Privacy—The Reader Service is committed to protecting your privacy. Our Privacy Policy is available online at www.ReaderService.com or upon request from the Reader Service.

We make a portion of our mailing list available to reputable third parties that offer products we believe may interest you. If you prefer that we not exchange your name with third parties, or if you wish to clarify or modify your communication preferences, please visit us at www.ReaderService.com/consumerschoice or write to us at Reader Service Preference Service, P.O. Box 9062, Buffalo, NY 14269. Include your complete name and address.

HII1

USA TODAY *bestselling author Lynne Graham*
is back with a thrilling new trilogy
SECRETLY PREGNANT, CONVENIENTLY WED

Three heroines must marry alpha males to keep
their dreams...but Alejandro, Angelo and Cesario
are not about to be tamed!

Book 1—JEMIMA'S SECRET
Available March 2011 from Harlequin Presents®.

JEMIMA yanked open a drawer in the sideboard to find
Alfie's birth certificate. Her son was her husband's child.
It was a question of telling the truth whether she liked it or
not. She extended the certificate to Alejandro.

"This has to be nonsense," Alejandro asserted.

"Well, if you can find some other way of explaining how
I managed to give birth by that date and Alfie not be yours,
I'd like to hear it," Jemima challenged.

Alejandro glanced up, golden eyes bright as blades and
as dangerous. "All this proves is that you must still have
been pregnant when you walked out on our marriage. It
does not automatically follow that the child is mine."

"'I know it doesn't suit you to hear this news now and I
really didn't want to tell you. But I can't lie to you about it.
Someday Alfie may want to look you up and get acquainted."

"If what you have just told me is the truth, if that little
boy does prove to be mine, it was vindictive and extremely
selfish of you to leave me in ignorance!"

Jemima paled. "When I left you, I had no idea that I was
still pregnant."

"Two years is a long period of time, yet you made no
attempt to inform me that I might be a father. I will want
DNA tests to confirm your claim before I make any deci-

sion about what I want to do."

"Do as you like," she told him curtly. "*I* know who Alfie's father is and there has never been any doubt of his identity."

"I will make arrangements for the tests to be carried out and I will see you again when the result is available," Alejandro drawled with lashings of dark Spanish masculine reserve.

"I'll contact a solicitor and start the divorce," Jemima proffered in turn.

Alejandro's eyes narrowed in a piercing scrutiny that made her uncomfortable. "It would be foolish to do anything before we have that DNA result."

"I disagree," Jemima flashed back. "I should have applied for a divorce the minute I left you!"

Alejandro quirked an ebony brow. "And why didn't you?"

Jemima dealt him a fulminating glance but said nothing, merely moving past him to open her front door in a blunt invitation for him to leave.

"I'll be in touch," he delivered on the doorstep.

What is Alejandro's next move? Perhaps rekindling their marriage is the only solution! But will Jemima agree?

Find out in Lynne Graham's
exciting new romance
JEMIMA'S SECRET

Available March 2011
from Harlequin Presents®.

Start your Best Body today with these top 3 nutrition tips!

1. **SHOP THE PERIMETER OF THE GROCERY STORE:** The good stuff—fruits, veggies, lean proteins and dairy—always line the outer edges of the store. When you veer into the center aisles, you enter the temptation zone, where the unhealthy foods live.

2. **WATCH PORTION SIZES:** Most portion sizes in restaurants are nearly twice the size of a true serving and at home, it's easy to "clean your plate." Use these easy serving guidelines:
   - Protein: the palm of your hand
   - Grains or Fruit: a cup of your hand
   - Veggies: the palm of two open hands

3. **USE THE RAINBOW RULE FOR PRODUCE:** Your produce drawers should be filled with every color of fruits and vegetables. The greater the variety, the more vitamins and other nutrients you add to your diet.

Find these and many more helpful tips in

YOUR BEST BODY NOW

by

TOSCA RENO

WITH STACY BAKER

Bestselling Author of
THE EAT-CLEAN DIET

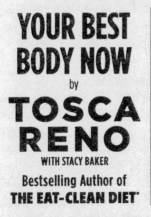

Available wherever books are sold!

NTRSERIESFEB